ID0788618

The Master Musicians Series

FRANCK

SERIES EDITED BY

SIR JACK WESTRUP
Professor Emeritus of Music, Oxford University
M.A., Hon.D.Mus.(Oxon.), F.R.C.O.

VOLUMES IN THE
MASTER MUSICIANS SERIES

THE MASTER MUSICIANS SERIES

FRANCK

by
LAURENCE DAVIES

*With eight pages of plates and
music examples in the text*

LONDON
J. M. DENT AND SONS LTD

OCTAGON BOOKS · NEW YORK

First published 1973
© Text, Laurence Davies 1973

Made in Great Britain
at the
Aldine Press · Letchworth · Herts
for
J. M. DENT & SONS LTD
Aldine House · Bedford Street · London

Library of Congress Catalog Card No. 73–53

ISBN: 0 460 03134 1

CONTENTS

PART I

PART II

ILLUSTRATIONS

Between pages 60 and 61

ACKNOWLEDGMENTS

IT is a somewhat Gilbertian situation when an author has to begin by acknowledging himself, but such is the circumstance under which this book was written that no other course is open to me. The fact is that in 1970 Messrs Barrie & Jenkins published my larger volume, *César Franck and His Circle*, on the understanding that they would have the option on subsequent works. At this point Messrs J. M. Dent unexpectedly asked me to do this Master Musicians book on Franck, an offer much too good to reject. To have gone ahead, however, would have been to contravene my previous agreement. Fortunately Barrie & Jenkins solved my dilemma by being generous enough to waive their objections on the condition that my work for them was suitably recognized. I therefore offer my first acknowledgment to this firm, declaring that any self-plagiarism that has occurred has been accidental and not deliberate. Certain facts about Franck's life are common property, and I could not very well avoid appropriating them once more. But otherwise this book is written in different language, draws its musical examples from different sources and considerably restricts the role enacted by 'the circle'.

Beyond this debt, I owe others scarcely less important. Rollo Myers provided me with some illustrations and much stimulating discussion on Franck. Other critics, who reviewed my previous book, made many constructive suggestions about my presentation of the subject. The bibliography, brief though it is, reveals how much I owe to the work of my predecessors. Naturally a large share of the gratitude must go to Sir Jack Westrup, editor of the series, and those members of the Dent staff who assisted the book on its way along the production line. Their advice and corrections have proved invaluable, even though I have no doubt retained my own mistakes in certain sectors. Finally, I have pleasure again in thanking my wife for her patience and tolerance, and for making it possible for me to get the necessary work done with the minimum of interruption.

L. D.

INTRODUCTION

ALMOST more than any other composer we care to name, César Franck (1822–90) epitomizes certain dilemmas of classification. There are some commentators who regard him as typically Belgian, others who shamelessly wave the tricolour of France above his name. A small minority insists that he was actually descended from the same Teutonic stock as his great organ-playing predecessors. Nationalist feelings obviously ferment easily in such a situation. Beyond this important problem lies one which is even more important. This is the problem of whether we should think of Franck purely and simply as a composer—of whatever nationality—and exclude the fact that he was a professor at the Paris Conservatoire and a teacher of practically unequalled gifts. The same might be alleged, the astute reader will say, of Cherubini, Massenet and Fauré. But Franck differed radically from these men in his ability to practise the Socratic art of eliciting brilliance from pupils of no more than average talent. Cherubini (much to his disgust) had Berlioz for his pupil; Massenet had Debussy; and Fauré had Ravel. Franck, on the contrary, laboured hard to teach musicians of lesser natural advantage such as d'Indy, Chausson and Duparc. And it is a tribute to his skill as a pedagogue that without him to instruct them these musicians might quite well not have entered the history books. Finally, we are left with the old teaser—not peculiar to Franck—of how best to judge a composer whose works bear signs of both haste and sluggishness and which range in merit from the puerile to the perfect.

Clearly one way in which the reader can be helped is by hacking out some sort of trail for himself in his pursuit of these and other pressing questions. The nationality issue is one that will be tackled factually in Chapter I. Its presence in this Introduction may be accounted for by reference to the part it plays in determining the composer's place in the musical tradition. This place was in Paris during the Second Empire and part of the Third Republic. Having lived almost all his life in the city, it was against corrupt French standards that Franck made his stand,

and towards the improvement of which that he devoted his efforts. His refusal to quit the capital during the Franco-Prussian War of 1870, along with his dedication to the church of Sainte-Clotilde, should be evidence of his loyalty to France. After all, he could easily have escaped to Belgium during the conflict (as his colleague Gounod did to England). However, he disdained to follow Fauré by retreating as far as Rambouillet, preferring to carry food and coal to aged Frenchmen beset by an enemy from whom he was considered to have sprung. Duparc's memories of his teacher at this time do not hint at treasonable thoughts or actions. Franck had no special affection for the greatest German composer of his day, namely Wagner, and he condoned the worship of Bayreuth by his numerous pupils without ever once setting foot in that town himself. The toxic effect *Tristan* had upon him is recorded in his own handwriting on the title-page of his score. True, Beethoven continued all his life to be a God-like presence, dwarfing all Frenchmen of the age. But this adulation on Franck's part was not peculiar to him. It was common among the intelligentsia of all nations, until the devastating Monsieur Croche—*alias* Debussy—revealed the proverbial feet of clay.

Franck's Belgian contacts were better preserved, partly because there can be no question that he lived and played there a great deal as a young man and left friends and relatives behind. Moreover other indisputably Belgian musicians took an interest in him. Without the goodwill of Eugène Ysaÿe, for instance, it is unlikely that Franck's Violin Sonata would have secured such an easy passage around the world. Ysaÿe was originally from Liège and was a founder of the famous 'Twenty Club' in Brussels. It is hard to interpret Franck's visits to the Théâtre de la Monnaie in that city as possible expressions of national pride, since it is well known that Parisians who had failed to get their works performed at the Opéra were more often than not compelled to seek the support of this house as their second choice. Franck's own operas were unworthy of production at either theatre, but he was adamant in his championship of the better-written works of d'Indy, Chabrier and his other French friends. It is understandable, therefore, that he should have wished to preserve what managerial contacts he had, and was unfortunate that he did not live to see them bear more fruit.

The issue of the musician as teacher or composer is naturally fraught

Introduction

with all kinds of complexities, and in Franck's case is further compli-
cated by an old-fashioned pedagogy against which he was compelled to
react at the Conservatoire where he was Professor of Organ from 1872.
Long before his elevation to these heights, however, Franck had been
immersed—perhaps too deeply—in the day-to-day function of instructing
others in the rudiments of musical theory and practice. His first steps in
the musical world—at the tender age of eight—were marked by a certain
academic precocity. They were made at Liège Conservatoire, and were
accompanied by two first prizes and a presentation copy of Meyerbeer's
opera *Robert le Diable*. True, the boy's grasping father wanted to with-
draw him from the seclusion of the classroom and force him instead to
don the mantle of the virtuoso, with the object of earning vast fees with
which to support the family. But Nicolas-Joseph Franck's dream of
fostering another Liszt was rudely shattered by a variety of factors—the
slowly changing climate of taste in Paris which, with one or two excep-
tions, favoured opera stars above pianists; César's own immaturity when
matched against a Marmontel or a Thalberg; and a gradual longing for
privacy which Nicolas-Joseph had not expected would emerge in his
son. These factors were unquestionably belated in revealing themselves,
with the result that the years 1836–46 were years of unhappy indecision.
What they proved was that the classroom, if not ideal, was at least more
propitious for César than the concert-hall. Although by this time composing had become an intermittent habit, he was more or less right in
assuming that the rest of his life would be indissolubly linked to
the educational mill and, of course, to the early morning church
service.

While it is possible to doubt the wisdom by which Franck embarked
on this pedestrian career, it would be unsound to imagine that he could
suddenly have switched to becoming a major composer, or to believe that
the public would have been favourable to him. Composers, like performers, were increasingly acclaimed in the opera-house, and were losing
ground in other sectors. This was especially true of France, where the
advent of Rossini and Meyerbeer had been regarded as a mandate for
consigning the chamber musician and the symphonist to a garret. Since
the retranslation of his memoirs we hardly need to be reminded of how
acute were Berlioz's struggles to gain a hearing for anything displaying

his unique flair for orchestration.[1] Meanwhile laudable attempts at developing an orchestral repertoire made by such latecomers as Saint-Saëns and Lalo were greeted with jeers and condescension. Usually entry to the key academic posts was effected through operatic triumphs. It is surely no coincidence that the nineteenth-century directors of the Conservatoire in Paris—Cherubini, Auber and Ambroise Thomas—were all theatrically renowned, and that it was only with Fauré's un-expected appearance in 1905 that such a powerful position fell to a man who up to that point had achieved no such popular acclaim. This situation meant that Franck, whose natural bent was towards the teaching and playing of instrumental music, was something of a prisoner even within the institutional citadel to which he belonged. The rebuffs and humiliations he endured (later to be avenged at the Schola Cantorum) will all be related in due course. For the moment it is sufficient to stress that the feebleness of the composer's early works was not so much due to his basic incompetence as to their containment within a more or less totally commercialized system.

Still it is obvious that Franck would have been a somewhat obscure composer even if everything had gone right for him. By this it may be concluded that he was no born genius, but rather ordinary as a young man with little besides a pronounced talent for the mechanics of his art. A sense of critical and philosophical values was not apparent in him till late in life, much of what should have been his best period being marked by banality or sterility. Indeed his entire career could be viewed as a dour, unspectacular effort to win fame in spheres in which it was not worth the winning, with only his last decade offering him the hope of a deserved immortality. As with Beethoven, it is feasible to divide his life into three periods, but in Franck's case it was simply the final period that won the interest of posterity. Eccentricity played an important role in the lives of both musicians, accounting to some extent for the unevenness to be found in their work and the fact that more of their personal foibles are to be detected in it. While d'Indy's tendency to equate the two composers in terms of ability can be emphatically rejected, it could be argued that they were both well ahead of their respective times and both disposed to

[1] *The Memoirs of Hector Berlioz*, translated by David Cairns (Gollancz, 1969).

frown on the frivolous and immoral.[1] Essentially they were serious men—Franck perhaps a shade solemn as well—but in their different ways they campaigned against complacency and mediocrity, somehow managing to imbue their music with a distinct sense of mission.

As we well know, Beethoven's struggles were directed against the condescension of the Viennese aristocracy and its tendency to reduce his art to mere elegance and formal symmetry. His inner struggles were related to the world of silence to which he had early been consigned. By contrast Franck's adversaries were the superficial operatic idols of the Second Empire and their fawning sycophants in the nation's conservatoires. His form of stoicism sprang from an almost evangelical devotion to love, harmony and industry. As the composer was a devout Catholic, very attached to his church duties, this devotion was fated to appear effusive to his superiors, to whom he inevitably seemed a trifle eccentric. Works like *Rédemption* and *Les Béatitudes* scarcely did much to enhance his standing with the authorities, and clearly had no place in the liturgy. They abandoned form for spirit. It must be said that such works exhibited no great genius, and that whereas it is easy to see why the *Missa Solemnis*, with all its awkward vocal writing, should have been hailed for the masterpiece of projected suffering it was, no such claim could honestly have been made on behalf of Franck's sacred compositions. Often unimaginative in conception, as well as poor in execution, they seem to vacillate uneasily between the secular and religious, or fail in their obligation to present us with the anguished emotions without which no redemption or beatific vision can have true meaning. It is therefore partly in Beethoven's greater spiritual awareness that we discover his superiority as a composer.

If, following the example of d'Indy, we divide Franck's career into the customary three periods, then it is insufficient simply to add the rider that it was only his third period that really mattered. The first and second periods display a formative, not to say biographical, importance which

[1] See Vincent d'Indy, *César Franck* (Paris, Alcan, 1906). A new paperback edition of the not wholly satisfactory translation by R. Newmarch is available in Constable's Dover Books series. It incidentally establishes that Bodley Head put out the first edition of this translation in 1910 and not 1909 as some critics have stated.

should not be overlooked. After all, they are what established the conditions in which the composer's best music came to be written. As we have already implied, the first period was one of pure precocity—theoretical and instrumental. No other assumption was made than that Franck would become a pianist. It was hardly a happy period, and it lasted from the middle of the 1830s—when Franck *père* summarily imposed on his son a grinding tour of the principal cities of Belgium—to the middle of the 1840s, when the boy's recitals began to suffer and his health to sink to a hazardous level. Even afterwards Nicolas-Joseph persevered with his prodigy for several more years, during which periods learning and teaching were interspersed with pursuit of the main objective. This became the point, too, at which César evidently yearned for a composer's existence. The whole phase came to an abrupt end with his marriage in 1848, an event virtually forced upon him by the sickening way of life he was enduring. From then on he made it plain that he was hankering after different aims from those his father had marked out for him, despite his conspicuous absence from the publishers' catalogues. Henceforth he was more reputed for his performances on the organ than on the piano, though he remained a good pianist. By contrast with his frustrated adolescence it was certainly a contented period of his life. It was not, however, his peak. Only after acquiring his chair, consolidating his circle and imbibing the spirit of the Third Republic could he be said to have attained this. Unhappily his maximum creative vigour and the acclaim accorded to him coincided with his unexpected death in 1890, when he was only sixty-eight.

Without delving too deeply into the reasons for his failure and the brief moment of his success, it seems obvious that Franck arrived on the scene too early to give much immediate assistance to the future of instrumental music in France and too late to enjoy the dividends so richly, and perhaps unfairly, heaped on the tigerish Liszt and Thalberg. As the son of a petty clerk he was in any case deprived of entry to the fashionable salons which might conceivably have made his name, and since he was not a particularly personable young man, equipped with romantic airs, it is hardly likely that he would have ensnared a countess or princess to assist him in his ambitions. To put it directly, he was a somewhat gauche and timid individual—almost his own worst enemy at a time when the arts remained the prerogative of the Hugos and the Lamartines, the Paganinis and the Malibrans, the followers of Delacroix and Géricault. An element of showmanship was unfortunately indispensable. The still more mundane nature of the composer's second period—which can be equated with the various church appointments he took up—was no doubt a product of the same reticence. At least the impression this period gives is one of extreme hesitancy. Acceptance of defeat as a performer was a pronounced symptom, and so was a certain lack of creative assertion. Many of the works written in this phase have an imitative look about them as though Franck were relying too heavily on the cheap-jack standards of the tastemakers. His unexpected elevation to academic honours may have been the occasion of his developing greater confidence, but it is more likely that the collapse of the Second Empire and all its cultural froth was a greater incentive for emerging from his self-imposed exile. By this time, too, he had one or two militant pupils, like d'Indy, to intercede on his behalf.

Oddly enough there are probably no other cases in musical history of such a slow development as Franck's. Psychologists are at liberty to explain this as a reaction to the unwelcome glare of publicity he was compelled to endure as a child—undeniably a traumatic experience in his life. But there is an equally good case to be made for regarding the composer as one of nature's basic introverts, to all intents and purposes quite normal, yet harbouring an acute fear and dislike of the cut-throat competition that was so marked a feature of the musical life of his times. It should be remembered, too, that for all his religious zeal he lived in an age when entrenched orthodoxy was being routed by Renan, Taine and their supporters. Having, as he did, limited intellectual resources, it is hard to imagine Franck embarking on his dramatic and programmatic works with the confidence of a Liszt or a Berlioz. Without religion as the inspiration of his talent, he was apt to slide into desultoriness or sloth. As we have seen, however, it was an oddly personalized religion that appealed to him, so that he became the loser whether or not the standard faith remained in the ascendant. At least his religious works pleased neither the devout nor the sceptics, while his tone-poems had not the sustained literary interest we normally associate with the genre. As opera and oratorio were the only really admired forms during the first half of

Franck's composing life, it is not even likely that he could have won outstanding success for himself with his tone-poems in Paris had he been endowed with a richer cultural background, as the case of Berlioz proved. To continue with his disappointing career as a teacher or *artisan d'église* was accordingly his sole outlet.

Historically what saved Franck from repeatedly composing works unsuited to his abilities was undoubtedly the fall of the Second Empire in 1870. Within two years of this event he had enlisted the aid of Saint-Saëns, Duparc and Bussine in founding the admirable Société Nationale de Musique, the object of which was to promote new French chamber-music and to resuscitate the habit of concert-going as opposed to evenings at the opera. Hence, at the unpropitious age of fifty, Franck had his first opportunity to write works of another kind altogether, along with a band of similarly deprived musicians, all of whom could look forward to hearing what they had written performed under the aegis of an efficient organization. The results were prolific all round. By the end of the new decade Franck had composed his Piano Quintet—unquestion-ably among his best works—and his symphonic poem, *Les Éolides*. Using these as precedents it took him only a few more years to embark on the remaining orchestral works, including *Le Chasseur Maudit* and ultimately the Symphony, and a wealth of brilliant essays for chamber ensemble or piano, among which the popular *Prélude, Choral et Fugue*, Violin Sonata and String Quartet have come to seem the most enduring. The last eighteen years of the composer's life consequently witnessed a spate of his own pupils' compositions which almost alone revived the nation's musical ideals.

Franck's pupils at the Conservatoire had by this time exercised such a pronounced effect upon his morale that it would be unjust to exclude them from whatever credit is deserved. D'Indy, as we have noted, worked tirelessly to promote the academic principles embraced in earlier times by Beethoven, and was to proceed after Franck's death to champion Rameau, Monteverdi, Marc-Antoine Charpentier and other forgotten geniuses at his Schola Cantorum, founded as an academy in 1896. At much the same point Duparc was assisting Fauré to develop the *mélodie*, or art-song, as a refined improvement on the outworn *romance*. Chausson, too, worked hard, if not always successfully, at this new medium, incorporating many of the techniques he had acquired from Franck and giving to them the publicity that only his wealth and social position could achieve. Other pupils—too numerous to recount—assisted in buttressing their teacher's none too secure position by forcing the public to accept small-scale works of high merit as a means of breaking the alternately grandiose and frivolous monopolies upon which France's musical claims had hitherto rested. Alexis de Castillon's Quintet and *Pièces dans le style ancien* came within this purview, as did the later and more intense works of Guillaume Lekeu, Franck's last pupil. Between these came a variety of well-intentioned supporters who must have imbued Franck with a large part of the determination that was to carry him so triumphantly into his last and most highly esteemed phase—musicians like Charles Bordes, Guy Ropartz, Louis de Serres and Pierre de Bréville. Each of these men, instead of clinging to Franck for protection, adopted the role of missionary, often venturing into the provinces of France to further his teaching.

Obviously it would be exceeding the function of this book to describe in detail the efforts of these followers; indeed I have done my best by them elsewhere.[1] Mention of them here merely serves to underline how much Franck depended on the security of comradeship, and how powerless he was to act without it. An essentially high-minded man, it would be going too far to assert that the composer was also heroic. The very opposite of his contemporary, Wagner, whom so many of his pupils admired, Franck possessed no real belief in the power of his genius to shake the world, and he singularly lacked the egoism that more often than not goes with the artistic temperament. Not only was he easily crushed by mediocre musicians, who either neglected or manhandled his scores, but he just as easily fell prey to the false advice given him by his family. And by this we refer not simply to his rapacious father. In later life even the composer's milder-mannered wife Félicité berated him cruelly for failing to achieve the commercial success for which he had so little desire, while his progressively minded son, Georges, with his brisk, domineering personality, bullied him into many an ill-advised venture. In his character, then, Franck must be viewed as paradoxical. As with

[1] See my *César Franck and His Circle*, Parts II & III (Barrie & Jenkins, 1970).

his music, he occasionally showed signs of timidity and conformity. Yet some kind of inner nobility prevented him from being docile or cowardly, and it was this quality that led to his characterization as the *Pater Sera-phicus*, or serene father of his flock. It was a role he was unable to play among his real family, but perhaps for that reason he was quick to assume it in the family of musical friends which by any count must be reckoned the true focus of his life.

Final briefing of the reader should be concerned with Franck's place in the history of music. Not trespassing on genuine liturgical ground, he can scarcely be considered a church musician in the creative sense. As a masterly exponent of long-neglected chamber forms he rather stakes a strong claim to neo-classical status, and this some fifty years before *Les Six*. Without him there could hardly have been a Magnard, a Dukas, a Roussel. Regarded alongside Liszt as a pioneer of the symphonic poem, it is also permissible to think of him as a late Romantic, a forerunner of Chausson and, more remotely, of such an apparently modern sensualist as Messiaen.

PART I

CHAPTER I

THE BELGIAN YEARS

To entitle our first chapter thus is to beg the obvious question, for we have yet to determine the precise nature of Franck's origins. That he was the elder (and not, as Winton Dean mistakenly concluded, the younger) son of Catherine and Nicolas-Joseph Franck, and that his name figured in the registry of births at Liège for 10th December 1822, are acknowledged facts. Equally indisputable is the claim that the composer was not officially entitled to describe himself as Belgian till he had reached the age of eight—the point at which his musical talent first manifested itself. This was because no Belgian state existed prior to 1830, only the Flemish and Walloon provinces being recognized, and these without sovereignty. Franck's city of Liège was sited in the Walloon district and pledged itself to the French crown. Most people in the city spoke good French, as they do today. Indeed its inhabitants will tell you, with some pride and a touch of exaggeration, that the Liègeois speaks the best French in the world. D'Indy was therefore correct, and not up to his usual nationalistic tricks, when he portrayed the locality of Franck's birth as 'peculiarly French . . . in sentiment and language'.[1] On the other hand it would certainly be misleading to convey the impression that the typical native of Liège differed little if at all from that of, say, Rouen or Nancy. Being so near the border, the Walloons had for a long time maintained cultural affinities with another nation, traditionally the enemy of France, which were bound to offset linguistic and other sympathies. Furthermore the issuing of the charter of independence at Franck's tender age of eight could not have failed to exert a considerable influence on his upbringing.

[1] D'Indy, *op. cit.*

I

Franck

It is interesting that the Walloons petitioned for independence just when they did. For it implies that they were (or liked to regard themselves as) political separatists. And their sturdy opinion of themselves found an outlet in their encouragement of the French to rebel against Louis-Philippe in 1848. Admittedly their alliance with their Flemish neighbours under King Leopold denied them republican status. But they were none the less antagonistic towards the *ancien régime* and opposed even the most benign efforts to reinstate it. As a young Belgian, then, Franck was reared on fairly liberal principles, though it is always worth remembering that his father was naturally among the first to subvert these if any profit was to be made from doing so. To that extent father and child could fairly be described as lackeys of the aristocracy whenever it suited the boy's career. A cultural historian would no doubt detect a moral in this, namely, that it was a mistake to try to revive the principle of private patronage after its day had passed. Certainly it was a mistake on Nicolas-Joseph's part, since none of his grovelling before the Belgian court or the privileged members of *tout Paris* did his son the slightest good as a charmer in the salons. Either the age of such romantics was past or else César's own miserableness put a damper on the idea. Still, it is of some consequence that the boy himself grew up amid progressive political thinking. For later in his life he was called upon on two occasions to declare his sympathies—once during the rebellion of 1848 and again during the more bloodthirsty Commune of 1871. His attitudes were deeply ambiguous.

But we have leaped ahead of our story, and the enigmatic circumstances of César's nationality have to be confronted once more before we can proceed with his career. We have said that he and his parents became Belgian in 1830. There are genealogists, however, who are inclined to doubt that they were ever fully Walloon in the first place. Franck is possibly a name of German origin, and Nicolas-Joseph's ancestors could quite possibly have belonged to that nation. As it was he was born at a little town called Gemmenich, a few miles from Aachen. His wife was definitely of German stock, and the possibility that the family moved in German circles is suggested by the fact that César himself had a rudimentary grasp of the language. (In church, for example, he was sometimes heard to murmur the words *Ich heile dich*.) In the case of

2

Nicolas-Joseph, however, it is easy to carry such speculations too far. There are records of a Franck at Liège going back to the sixteenth century—a court appointment as a stained-glass window craftsman being granted by Henri III to one Jérôme Franck, an alleged forbear of César's who lived there at that time. It is plausible, therefore, to assume that the composer's relatives on his father's side had been scattered throughout the Netherlands and not Germany.

Emmanuel Buenzod, in his recent study of the composer, none the less confirms that a branch of the family sprang up at Aachen, adding that the family habitually spoke 'low German'.[1] However, he still seems to regard the notion that Franck was essentially German as untenable. Jean Gallois, another French biographer, reminds us of how d'Indy and Paul de Wailly (a later Franck pupil with a pronounced interest in dialect) discussed the possibility of their teacher being *un peu Picard*; and of how Debussy would refer to him as *un musicien flamand*.[2] Gallois certainly seems to have uncovered some remote German ancestors on the paternal side in identifying first one Léonard Franck, who emigrated to Germany in 1459, and a century later a Jan Franck, who held a position as Director of the Imperial Mines at Calamine in Moresnet. It is evident that this individual had connections with Holland and Prussia, and it was from his strain of the family that the Gemmenich Francks stemmed. The Dutch element, of course, adds the possibility of a further complication. Since Nicolas-Joseph's father died when he was two it is not possible to get more reliable information.

Catherine, or to give her her full name, Marie-Catherine-Barbe, was six years older than Nicolas-Joseph whom she met at her native Aachen. Their courtship lasted two years, and they were married on 20th August 1820, afterwards taking an apartment near Sainte-Croix in Liège. A clerk by profession, Nicolas-Joseph had broken with the clerical-ecclesiastical tradition of which his family must once have been part, though 13 Rue St Pierre, Liège, where César was born and grew up, was within viewing distance of the churches of St André and St Paul as

[1] Buenzod, *César Franck*, in the series *Musiciens de tous les temps* (Paris, Éditions Seghers, 1966).

[2] Gallois, *César Franck*, in the *Solfèges* series (Paris, Éditions du Seuil, 1966).

well as the Prince-Bishop's palace. The profusion of Christian names with which he was inflicted was not uncommon in those days, though in his case an attempt seems to have been made to mix humble family pride with monarchical grandeur. He was actually christened César-Auguste-Guillaume-Hubert. Not surprisingly a diminutive version appeared on his concert programmes, though César-Auguste Franck de Liège hardly erred on the side of modesty. Probably these lofty names reflected Nicolas-Joseph's grandiose vision of the Franck family's future. The excuse he offered for César's professional designation was that he should not be confused with the composer Eduard Franck of Berlin. But, since neither was exactly knocking on the door of fame, it is more probable that snobbery and ambition were the real motives.

The younger son Joseph was not considered to have his brother's high talent, though his prowess on the violin led to the proposal that they should be encouraged to give joint recitals. Joseph, named after his father, took on many of Nicolas-Joseph's traits. For instance he was ruthlessly ambitious and strove to give the impression that he was growing up to be something of a paragon. Nicolas-Joseph, however, was aware that a considerable discrepancy existed between the abilities of his children, and when the time came he intended that César should ride the tide of fortune while Joseph should settle down to a more humdrum career as a music-teacher. As we shall see, affairs did not work out quite as ex-pected. César's failure to fulfil the ideal of top-flight virtuoso was as surprising as Joseph's conviction that what his brother had lacked he himself possessed—with the paradoxical result that, by the time the boys were out of their teens, it was Joseph who was to be found pressing on with the aim of concert executant and his far more gifted, if retiring, brother who had thrown in his hand. However, while Nicolas-Joseph's hopes were pinned on his eldest son, he spent almost all his time in the role of unpaid impresario. In 1834, while César was still a promising pupil at the Royal Liège Conservatoire, his father risked a tour of Belgium, including Brussels, where King Leopold was given an opportunity to hear the youngster play. It is hardly surprising that the opportunity yielded naught, since at that time he was competing, in the customary Romantic fashion, with a variety of well-known artists—

including Malibran and her sister Pauline Viardot,[1] and subsequently the notable pianist Marmontel.

While young César Franck was being required to show off his skill before these more experienced performers it was inevitable that he would arouse little notice. Still, his father was not a man to be easily discouraged. He secured lessons for his son from Zimmermann (Marmontel's teacher), and after several costly attempts to launch his career in Paris (including one especially disastrous recital at the huge Gymnase Musical which, to judge from the following day's press, must have been half filled with bored or hostile music critics and hardly anyone else) he made the crucial decision to move to the French capital with a view to entering his offspring at the larger Conservatoire. This decision was crucial in more than one respect. To begin with it meant that he, Nicolas-Joseph, would have to take out French citizenship again if César were to stand much chance of admission. Secondly, it involved another long period of study for the boy, whose interests would as likely as not be further deflected from the concert-hall to the study. This latter thought probably did not cross Nicolas-Joseph's mind. On the first point it is essential to underline the fact that the assumption of French citizenship—coming so closely after being pronounced Belgian—complicates still further the nationality issue. Of course it was not César who was applying for a change of status, but as he was still a minor it amounted to very much the same thing. At any rate this was the course followed, Nicolas-Joseph being granted what he desired after putting in a short period of residence, and César being admitted to Cherubini's famous institution on 4th October 1837.[2] Predictably César found his

[1] Malibran, one of the century's greatest singers and a particular favourite of Berlioz's, died in her twenties; but her sister Pauline lived to a great age, becoming renowned during the early days of the Third Republic for her association with the Russian novelist Turgenev and for playing hostess to a galaxy of celebrities. It was her daughter Marianne who attracted Fauré so much and who was alleged to have inspired such relatively late works as the *Requiem* after their broken engagement.

[2] Some qualification is necessary here, for Franck himself was obliged to sign residential papers much later in life—in 1872 when he won his professorship—committing him further to French nationality. The question thus remains complex and open to interpretation.

new surroundings much to his liking. Exhausting tours were, for the moment, in abeyance, and instead he found himself bombarded with those exercises in harmony and counterpoint that most students regard as their despair but which César responded to with joy.

It was not as if he had lacked all French academic precedent in music. Aside from the Zimmermann lessons he had also been permitted to study composition with the Czech immigrant, Antonín Reicha, in 1835; and since Reicha was on the Conservatoire's staff many tales about it had probably filtered through. At a guess, some of these would have been pretty unfavourable, for Reicha was much too progressive to have been popular with his colleagues. A mystic who read Kant and advocated startling harmonic procedures (polytonality among them), it is not too difficult to see in Reicha the father César substituted for the abhorrent Nicolas-Joseph. At least no one will deny that in later life two of Franck's most pronounced musical characteristics were a love of transcendentalism in religious composition (e.g. *Rédemption, Les Béatitudes*) and a fondness for audacious modulation. It is even possible that the composer's reverence for Beethoven may have taken root from Reicha, the two having matriculated together at Bonn. It was a pity for Franck that Reicha died after a very brief acquaintance. One feels that he would have been able to direct the young Belgian prodigy's career with far greater wisdom than any of the Conservatoire's typical professors. Unfortunately by the time César was installed as an official pupil at the institution this kind old philosopher had died, disappointed at the failure of his opera *Natalie*. Almost certainly one can make too much of the Franck-Reicha relationship, César being far too young to have grasped the full consequences of the other man's thought. But there is no doubt that he learned how to write a good fugue from Reicha, and that is something at which few matched him.

César's teachers at the Conservatoire were Habeneck, Leborne and Le Couppey. He managed to continue with the harsh Zimmermann for piano and eventually he found his way into François Benoist's classes for organ. A wide range of influences was therefore brought to bear on him. Habeneck's orchestral concerts (at which Berlioz had already had a nerve-shattering experience) must surely have furnished Franck with much-needed knowledge of the repertory.[1] Leborne, on the other hand, taught him about the violin—of which instrument he assuredly displayed a compositional mastery in later life. Le Couppey's influence was probably negligible, but Benoist had the curious honour of both helping to make and unmake Franck as an organist, the role in which Rongier was to portray him and the public forever to view him. This was because Benoist straddled the two great ages of French organ-playing without ever exemplifying either. Born too late to have built up a tradition based on Bach's use of the baroque organ, he was too old for the innovations of technique posed by the new 'symphonic' organ of which Lefébure-Wély, Lemmens and ultimately Widor were to be the uncrowned kings. Many of these innovations resulted from the work of Cavaillé-Coll, whose life was spent in the company of men like Franck and Saint-Saëns, restoring and building instruments in the 1850s and 1860s. It was he who built the Sainte-Clotilde organ upon which Franck doted for the remainder of his days.[2] Being younger than Benoist, yet obliged to learn from him, Franck surprisingly had a somewhat nebulous training in his favourite instrument, and had to learn, for instance, how to pedal effectively and how to use all the new stops (e.g. Cavaillé-Coll's famous clarinet stop) once the character of the instrument took on a full Romantic flavour.

As a matter of interest, Franck did rather better at piano than at the organ while at the Paris Conservatoire. At least he was awarded a *Grand Prix d'Honneur* for the former—a prize specially created for him because of his mildly impudent trick of transposing down a third the material given as a sight-reading test. The judges were impressed by this feat, but also a trifle piqued. They accordingly paid him a left-handed compliment in return. When it came to the organ, however, those in authority apparently failed to see that Franck had tried a similar ruse—this time combining the themes set for sonata and fugal extemporization

[1] According to the *Memoirs (op. cit.)*, Berlioz had to rescue the 'Tuba mirum' of his *Requiem* or *Grande Messe des Morts* from Habeneck's unsuccessful attempts to juggle with baton and snuff-box at one and the same time.

[2] Cavaillé-Coll has nowhere had the appreciation he really deserves as an organ-builder. It was he who influenced Henry Willis in building the Albert Hall organ, now under possible sentence of death.

—and simply awarded him second place. Each of these harmless attempts to thumb the nose at academicism seems out of character in a way. After all, César had cowered beneath his father's will for as long as anyone could recall, and he undoubtedly wanted to succeed educationally. Perhaps they should be construed as ingrained habits of showmanship which his father had always instilled in him; or merely efforts to draw attention away from the actual finish of his execution towards what may be called pedagogical humour. Franck was by all accounts not very adept at any other kind of humour, and several of the more honest pupils have testified that the composer was by no means superior as a player. Maurice Emmanuel, for example, thought him something less than first-rate as an organist, and Saint-Saëns, though not a pupil, would certainly not have regarded him as a virtuoso pianist. Though the composer generally gave the premières of his organ works himself there is no record of his having done so with the more important piano works; Louis Diémer, Mme Bordes-Pène, Mlle Marie Poitevin and Saint-Saëns himself all being made to stand in for him on one occasion or another. Prize-winning seems to require a special sort of temperament, however, and the fact that it took Franck three tries to obtain a first in counterpoint—a subject in which he could scarcely have been faulted in comparison with the average contender—suggests that he did not possess it. Perhaps it is worth remarking that those pupils who professed to love Franck most, or appeared to have most in common with him, also fell into this habit of getting themselves torpedoed in competitions and examinations. The prodigious Lekeu, for example, comes to mind with his fiasco over the Belgian *Prix de Rome*, while one cannot imagine Duparc ever getting as far as to complete an entry form.

After he had been at the Conservatoire three or four years Franck appeared nevertheless to be doing extraordinarily well. Cherubini liked him, as much as it was possible for him to like any of his students, and he had, albeit in an unorthodox fashion, collected a few major awards. At this point his ambition was directed, as was that of every good class-mate, towards the winning of the *Prix de Rome*, which would have meant three years' free tuition and lodgings at the Villa Medici. Franck's friend Gounod had triumphed, and it was confidently being predicted that he would do the same. What he did not know was that Nicolas-

Joseph had been watching his progress with less than fatherly pleasure. He had perceived that César was not about to eclipse Liszt. But what if his compositions turned out to be masterly? Italy did not materialize and even France became an object of farewell. For it was at this most critical stage of Franck's career that Nicolas-Joseph made what was unquestionably his major blunder by summarily withdrawing his son from the Conservatoire and coercing him back into the role of itinerant musician. The means were to be the same—more concert-giving in Belgium—only the end slightly different. Unfortunately for César he had embarked on a series of four Trios at about this time, and though he had previously turned out fantasies on the well-known operatic airs of the day (and other unpretentious creative exercises), this time he had gone far enough to implant a new suggestion in his father's mind. If indeed the boy were a young Mozart, what possible advantage was to be gained from locking him up in an academy for a further few years however distinguished it might be? César accordingly never learned whether or not he could have won the *Prix de Rome*. He was hustled back to Belgium before the contest was held.

With four commendable years of study behind him the young man (for he was now no longer in his teens) had cause to be furious. Instead he calmly resigned himself to his fate, wondering what tactics his father would use to buttress his new ambition. He soon found out. With his keen memory of King Leopold's attendance at one of Franck's former concerts, the road to be taken was obvious. Nicolas-Joseph had to discover a way of re-arousing the king's interest, this time with the prospect of helping to make a great Belgian composer. Grétry had come from Liège. Why not a composer of graver character? In a bizarre way Franck's father had caught hold of a valuable idea. It was his method of proceeding with it that was at fault. As it happened, few continental composers, other than Germans and Austrians, had bothered with chamber music for a century and more. Genuine returns were to be had from the idea that Belgium (or for that matter, France) might resurrect the duos, trios and quartets that had been popular in baroque and classical times. Undoubtedly too much attention had been given to opera and operetta, and it remains immensely to Franck's credit that— along with Saint-Saëns, Lalo and a few others—he devoted himself to the resuscitation of these outmoded forms. Whether or not the composer allowed himself to be influenced by the delicate *agréments* of Couperin or Leclair, or else by the more robust tonal assertions of Beethoven, remains an open question. Almost certainly the latter, one would suppose. The Trios Op. 1 will be analysed in their proper place. Here it is sufficient to state that Nicolas-Joseph's plan was to get them published in a limited edition under royal patronage.

Such a scheme was obviously very bold. Had it not been for Liszt's visible enthusiasm for the Fourth Trio (actually the longish last move-ment of the Third as it then stood) it is doubtful if the one hundred and seventy musicians whom Schlesinger, the engraver, describes would have consented to pay the subscription price of twelve francs which Nicolas-Joseph was proposing to set against the typical retail figure of forty-five. Among the subscribers were to be found Meyerbeer, Chopin, Halévy and, curiously, d'Indy's paternal grandmother, the Comtesse Rézia, whose son Wilfrid d'Indy had by a remarkable coincidence consulted Franck at Liège, going on to take a brief series of lessons with him in 1842. Commercially the Trios were by no means a disaster in the form in which they were issued. They did not, however, secure the royal imprimatur. Neither did they ever receive the royal performance which had been half-heartedly promised. Probably the royal family was bored with the entire project. All that Franck and his father got for their pains was a Gold Medal struck in the former's honour in 1843—an easy sop to the monarchical conscience. Greater zest was apparent in Germany, where the firm of Schuberth put out the works in an ordinary edition. This might have done well had Mendelssohn lived, for he was much taken with them. As things turned out, Liszt had to give the premières at Weimar in 1853, being followed by Ludwig Hermann in 1861. Von Bülow wrote Franck an extremely gratifying letter about them, though this came too late to provide much consolation, and Peter Cornelius was also alert to their possibilities. It was a tragedy that no real sponsor was found in France, for it was there if anywhere that a resurgence of interest in chamber music was desperately needed. Incredibly Franck's Trios were written in 1840, yet were not followed by any first-rate chamber works till the foundation of the Société Nationale thirty years later. These were lean years for Franck, and he almost failed to survive them.

CHAPTER II

CLOISTER AND HEARTH

THE gradual petering out of Franck's Belgian reputation meant that his father was obliged to return to Paris in 1844, taking the family with him, and hoping that perseverance would succeed where arrogance had failed. Still torn by doubts as to whether he should bill César as a performer or composer, Nicolas-Joseph now developed his managerial instincts to their utmost and even added to his other functions those of advertisement officer and ticket agent. It was at this point, however, that Franck's recitals began to suffer most unfairly from the attentions of the critic Blanchard, whose official standing with the *Gazette Musicale* and *Revue Musicale* was such that all candidates for public advancement were required to seek his approval. His predecessor on the latter journal, Maurice Bourges, had been just, if a little discouraging, in his treatment of César. At least he had appreciated that the young man was being exploited by his father and was going through the agonies of choosing between two careers. Bourges had not greatly admired the Trios (comparing them, strangely enough, with Ann Radcliffe's Gothic novels), but he was disinclined to use his position as a battering ram. Blanchard, however, was different—one of those critics to whom denigration and devastation were comforting words. His biting comments, coupled with the tired complaints of less spiteful writers who had none the less put up for too long with Nicolas-Joseph's unsubtle manœuvres, were what crushed the last vestiges of hope for fame in the decade that lay ahead. Joseph, as we know, carved out an independent path for himself—mostly in Belgium as a hopeless hanger-on in court circles—and 1st June 1846 was the final date in which the two opposed brothers appeared together in Paris. It was incidentally César's farewell as a performer on a public platform, if we discount the few occasions on which he later introduced one or two of his own works at festivals or the unpublicized occasions on which he indulged in a provincial organ recital.

Perhaps more unsettling for Franck than either the end of his career as a performer or the breaking-up of his partnership with his brother was the unexpected nervous collapse he had at the end of it all. Since he was known among his friends for the stability of his constitution it must have taken a great deal of pressure for this to happen to him. To account for his breakdown in the most complete way it is necessary to get some sort of picture of the life he was compelled to endure during the period when he was giving intermittent concerts and receiving increasingly damaging reviews. So that the family income would not suffer in this period Nicolas-Joseph forced his son to accept a truly mountainous load of teaching. In addition to having the use of a studio on Sunday afternoons in the Rue Montholon César was made to trudge from one school or college to another giving peripatetic lessons in the theory and practice of music. The Collège de Vaugirard, a Jesuit foundation dedicated to the Immaculate Conception, was one of these institutions, and a highly significant one, since it was there that the composer eventually en-countered his pupils Coquard and Duparc. Rollin was another stopping place on several days of the week. Franck's time-table, to put it in modern terms, was back-breaking, and the modest fees he collected went im-mediately to pay the expenses of his father's botched publicity campaigns. It was symptomatic that Franck never complained directly about this work as many a more flamboyant composer would have done. Up to a point he enjoyed teaching, and it was only the low level and high amount of it that drove him to despair.

That he did manage to struggle on, in a desultory way, with his com-position at this time is evidence that he had not utterly capitulated. Songs like *Le Sylphe* and *Robin Gray* appeared in 1843, and it might have been surmised that he would go on writing in this genre for the remainder of the decade. But even in the great age of the *mélodie* (which Duparc did so much to foster) Franck contributed little to the form. His under-standing of prosody was far too sketchy. What did interest him, however, was the possibility of setting, in a less metrical fashion, a quasi-religious ode of some sort. Félicien David, for instance, had had con-siderable success with his oriental fantasia, *Le Désert*, which Gustave Bertrand had enthused over in the pages of *Le Ménéstrel* and which had taken most of Paris by storm. David was a rather weak, pictorial composer, but he had somehow caught the prevailing mood—which was for something mildly exotic and yet able to please the fussiest clerics by its good taste. The subject Franck chose was the biblical story of Ruth. Possibly he had seen Poussin's much-admired painting of the meeting with Boaz. Conversely he might have been inspired by Gounod's gentle advice, for it was about this time that the future composer of *Faust* was perversely beginning his career by petitioning for holy orders—a sacrifice he was unable to make, but which he ever afterwards alluded to as a testimonial to his theological leanings. It need hardly be added that France had traditionally been intrigued by stories and parables of the East, ranging from Persia to China,[1] and a full-scale eclogue, with soloists, choir and orchestra and running to three parts, seemed a sure way of propelling Franck into the forefront of the nation's composers.

Ruth took about a year to write. It was begun in the autumn of 1844 and secured its rather singular première at the Salle Érard on 1st November 1845, just two months following its completion. Though not often mentioned in the catalogue of Franck's works, it cost its composer heroic labour and brought him bitter disappointment. Indeed its failure knocked the stamina out of him for most of his first period as a composer. By comparison his other calamities were anticipated, being greeted with stoicism and a far keener sense of the injustices of art. The interesting point about *Ruth* was that it was first of all presented as a private affair to which Nicolas-Joseph had invited a number of carefully selected musicians. These were all celebrities, and included Meyerbeer, Spontini, Halévy, Alkan, Heller, Moscheles, Adam, Liszt and the German pianist and organist Kuhn. The idea behind this strange proceeding was that unsympathetic critics as well as the general public might be excluded, while those invited could be made to feel that their status was being duly acknowledged. It all seemed clever enough in theory. But critics incline to be sharper in their remarks when any attempt is made to bar them from an event, and the general public as a rule only asserts

[1] Readers should scarcely require reminding of Montesquieu's *Lettres Persanes* and their unusual popularity. Neither should visitors to Versailles have forgotten the wealth of *chinoiserie* that reposes there. Later on orientalism was taken up in literature by Loti and Verhaeren, and in music by Saint-Saëns, Henri Rabaud, Bizet, Roussel, Ravel and many others.

its opinion of what it has heard. Consequently when Franck's father took steps to secure a second hearing under less stringent conditions at the hall of the Conservatoire on 4th January 1846, he did not reckon with a more or less ignorant public and a coldly aggrieved press.

After the Salle Érard concert things naturally looked rosy. The old stalwarts of French music displayed their good manners by dropping a few words of praise for the young composer whose work they had been specially privileged to hear, Liszt in particular indulging in one of his notoriously generous flourishes. When the Conservatoire performance came around, therefore, it was ardently hoped by César and his relatives that the word had spread as to the splendours in store for the people. Unhappily no such splendours made themselves felt, the average reaction being one of boredom. The indefatigable Blanchard (whom we might well name the Hanslick of Paris to young Franck's Bruckner) was not satisfied to write a merely dull report for his column. Like the malicious, insecure figure he was, he did not rest content until he had attacked Franck's composition from almost every angle in his vocabulary: The nobility of theme was one that Méhul could have treated with infinitely more dignity; melodically there was nothing to whet the appetite *à la* Rossini; passion was conspicuous by its absence. These were only the main charges. That they tended to contradict one another apparently did not matter. As with so many notices the object seemed to be to prove the composer unequal to the best in each sector. Méhul was the master of decorum, so Franck fell behind on that score. On the other hand, he was compared unfavourably with Rossini, the accepted master in tunefulness. Likewise it was bluntly implied that he was not in Meyer⁄beer's class as an instrumentalist or David's as an illustrator. Whether or not all these qualities were demanded by the work, or whether or not Franck showed himself a good runner⁄up in some of them, were ques⁄tions left unanswered. Actually, as Gallois has pointed out, *Ruth* was unique in avoiding the Italian banalities of the day, whatever other faults it was possible to find with it.[1] But Franck was never told this, and it took him a quarter of a century to lick the wounds he had received in this his first major foray.

[1] *op. cit.*

Cloister and Hearth

A singer from the Opéra-Comique, a Mlle Lavoye, sang the part of *Ruth* in this second production, and she was accompanied by seventy choristers and an orchestra of twenty-seven. Tilmant, director of the Théâtre Italien, took charge of the event after consultations with Habeneck at the Société des Concerts. The Duc de Montpensier was allegedly present at the performance, and this gave rise to rumours that further performances might take place at the court of Louis-Philippe. Nicolas-Joseph naturally gave wider currency to such rumours in the hope that they might thereby come true. But nothing other than gossip lay behind them and no subsequent performance of *Ruth* occurred until 1871 at the Cirque des Champs Élysées, by which time its initial failure had already taken its toll of the composer's health. At that point he even summoned the detachment necessary to make a few badly needed alterations, also allowing Hartmann to issue the work in a setting for voice and piano. D'Indy behaved in apoplectic fashion during this second public hearing, for he was aware that certain critics who had vilified the first were under the mistaken apprehension that they were listening to a new composition. Their greater charity infuriated him. However, his anger was largely wasted since none of them had the good grace to admit to having committed a *faux-pas*. The only consoling thought to emerge from the Salle Érard première was that Liszt showed himself sincerely and deeply impressed, writing that he considered Franck one of the three greatest composers in the country.[1] It is, of course, a matter open to doubt whether or not Nicolas-Joseph wormed this opinion out of him with the object of hastening a revival. Yet Liszt was almost always effusive over Franck's music—even in later years—perhaps recognizing that he owed a little of his religious romanticism to him. In any case his commendation of the Trios, along with his decision to choose the same subject for a symphonic poem, lends credibility to his sentiments.

Time will later be found for a scrutiny of the main sections of *Ruth*, one or two of which achieved an independent popularity as the century wore on. Significantly these tended to be the choral numbers. Possibly

[1] The letter in which Liszt recorded this opinion was written to the friend of Comte de Montalivet, *Ministre et Intendant de la Liste Civile*, so it is plausible that, notwithstanding his sincerity, he was also responding to a plea for canvassing.

the feeling that these represented the composer at his best was what led him to turn his thoughts in the direction of large-scale oratorio. At any rate, despite a brief excursion into the domain of organ composition, it was massed vocal writing that occupied him throughout the bulk of his second, somewhat febrile, creative period. The influences that went into the writing of *Ruth* (aside from David) were probably Schubert, Halévy and Meyerbeer—a very motley collection. No doubt they account for the alternately lyrical and bombastic styles discernible in Franck's first really ambitious opus. Despite its weaknesses, and its undoubted failure at the time of being written, *Ruth* embodied all the talent and hopes its composer was then able to muster. As Gallois has written : '*Ruth* perhaps represents the summation of Franck's dramatic talents at the age of twenty-four, but we are forced to admit that these talents were rather wan.'[1] Since the work has still not been recorded in its entirety it is conjectural to claim that it was a mistake to have attempted it. As with the other choral works, *Ruth* gave Franck valuable experience at writing for larger numbers and the equally necessary experience of learning to live with failure. The most obvious error on his part—and this applies to all his religious works—is that no effort seems to have been made to vary the tone, to mingle that vague community of sentiment which he took for love with the more vicious or passionate appetites of which we know man to be capable.

The consequence of *Ruth*'s disappearance from the concert-platform was a renewed urge to earn money by teaching. This urge was once more fostered by Nicolas-Joseph, dismay and frustration now constituting his only motives. Precisely on that account the schedule planned for Franck became insurmountably overloaded. Full-time composing was not to be possible, even if he had regained the mind to engage in it. The years 1846–8 accordingly saw him trundling once more through the streets of Paris from school to school, adding pupil after pupil to enlarge Nicolas-Joseph's meagre hoard. In 1847, probably after talking it over with Gounod, Franck nevertheless began to think hard about another project —this time a symphonic poem to be based on Victor Hugo's verses. The title, *Ce qu'on entend sur la montagne*, is identical with the first of Liszt's

[1] *op. cit.*

dozen or so essays in the genre, and on inspection is found to emanate from the same literary source. What this conveys to the musicologist is embarrassingly difficult to make clear. Questions of precedence and even plagiarism can easily arise. By most accounts, Liszt embarked on his own work later, though he conceived it very much earlier. Franck, on the other hand, actually started writing the moment he thought of it but in spite of putting the finishing touches to it before his rival he failed to find a publisher. The upshot was that Liszt, who was also tardy in breaking into print, got his version performed in 1849 and finally issued in 1852. At this later point Franck was still without an offer, and once it became obvious that Liszt was launched with the public and the music houses he ceased to take any further steps. No one knew, therefore, until 1870 or thereabouts that the composer had been close to inventing the form that in the meantime had so busily occupied Saint-Saëns, to say nothing of the many non-French Romantics of the mid-century. By then Liszt had run the gamut of popular subjects, including *Hamlet*, and had very nearly reached the end of his production, while Franck's own pupils Duparc and d'Indy had virtually caught him up (if one is allowed to think of the first panel of the *Wallenstein* trilogy as a symphonic poem in the making). His *Ce qu'on entend sur la montagne* was consequently left unpublished and unheard of.

There is very little point in disputing the respective claims of Liszt and Franck to this work and to the invention of the symphonic poem in general. On the former score many explanations could be made to hold water. For instance either man could have mentioned the subject to the other during their occasional meetings (the earliest going as far back as Franck's first Belgian tours) or in their not infrequent correspondence. No record of such a discussion exists, but that proves nothing. On the second score—and this is possibly more important—it is arguable that works resembling symphonic poems existed before either Franck or Liszt came to the fore. Overtures without operas (or even with operas) fulfil many of the conditions of a symphonic poem, which may be taken to mean a literary programme treated freely under orchestral conditions of short duration. If this much is conceded then Beethoven, Berlioz and Mendelssohn propose themselves as prior contenders, not to mention Weber. What seems so unfortunate is that the reputations of all these other composers were established without the genre in question. Franck, on the contrary, was here using it to make what could easily have been a final despairing gesture. It is more the pity since this work actually contained distinct merits that his previous works had lacked.

Probably the chief of these was his new-found ability to score effectively for the orchestra. Criticism of the composer for the ineptitude of his handling of instruments other than the organ and piano was not to cease with this work. Indeed the most full-blooded criticism coincided with the time when his compositions reached a wider public. This apparent paradox becomes explicable once we realize that Franck's development as a composer was not so much linear as distressingly zigzag. *Ce qu'on entend sur la montagne* has a certain lightness of touch and a prophetic manner of separating groups of instruments which are then pitted against one another with a pleasing effect of contrast. Critics hostile to the composer were only too ready to attribute this habit (which recurs in many of the more frequently played works of the middle period) to the typical organist's tendency to use instruments as if they were stops— waiting, as it were, for them to be pulled and for the putative changes of manual. But this explanation, while it could have been used to belittle some scores of the late period, is hardly credible when applied to works written before the wide range of revolutionary organ devices which were not to appear until the 1860s. A more plausible explanation is that Franck was a very unpredictable orchestrator throughout the whole of his career—some comparatively late works, like *Rédemption*, seem to be badly in need of retouching, while one or two earlier ones, such as this abortive symphonic poem, show quite a fair degree of competency. It is possible that Franck copied the style of this work from Spohr's programme-symphony, *Irdisches und Göttliches in Menschenleben*, a composition dating from 1841 which also deals with the distinction between nature and mankind, the opposed poles of Franck's essay.

In d'Indy's catalogue of the composer's works, this particular specimen is listed as the *Le Sermon sur la Montagne*, and since it met with such a withering reception was mistakenly assumed to be part of an early sketch for *Les Béatitudes*. Franck himself must therefore have been exceedingly reserved on the subject, and it is chiefly due to Léon Vallas, a later biographer, that we have an accurate account of the genesis of the matter.[1] Other longer-lived disciples than d'Indy, however, must have been aware of the obscurity surrounding the work. Indeed at the time of writing his last four symphonic poems in the 1870s and 80s it must have seemed to Franck's pupils that he had devoted a disproportionate share of his time to this genre. They doubtless inquired about its inception. D'Indy, for once a shade more critical than the others, thought rather poorly of the symphonic poem as a form—even though he perversely obliged posterity by writing several. Probably he considered it beneath a man of Franck's stamp to waste too much effort on what he would have regarded as literary frivolities. He held this view because, unlike the rest of the circle, he always seemed determined to see Franck as the heir of Beethoven, a supreme genius not sent into the world to fritter away his gifts on entertainment. His coldly disapproving attitude over *Psyché*—the last of the four works—was typical. The error he made over *Ce qu'on entend sur la montagne* may consequently have resulted from the fact that he did not really want to know of Franck's genuine enthusiasm for the new form.

To return to the 1840s, it is evident that among the deserts of boredom which were Franck's to tread, certain tiny oases of happiness now and again presented themselves. The chief of these was his regular visit at the house of M. and Mme Desmousseaux, an actor and actress at the Comédie Française. These were only their stage names, their marriage certificate being in the name of Saillot. The Desmousseaux had been in the theatre for several generations on Madame's side, her father having been the famous French performer referred to as Baptiste. When this veteran died he inadvertently bequeathed many of his roles to his son-in-law. At the moment of Franck's meeting with them they were exceedingly popular in Paris and attracted a gay and fairly uninhibited circle of friends. Much more significantly they had a daughter called Félicité, who, it was their intention, should take music lessons. Franck offered himself as the obvious man for the job. As time progressed a very amicable, even intimate, arrangement sprang up between him and the family. Mme Desmousseaux, anxious to foster an alliance between teacher and pupil, offered Franck the hospitality of her house in the Rue

[1] Vallas, *La Véritable Histoire de César Franck* (Paris, Flammarion, 1955).

Blanche in which to do a little composing—something firmly forbidden while on duty. This was followed by a surreptitious spell of courting, also unknown to the normally inquisitive Nicolas-Joseph. The outcome of it all—completely unsuspected by anyone outside the conspiracy—was that Franck had found himself a bride and without difficulty won the approval of her parents. It was his own family that provided César with the real test of his manliness, for Nicolas-Joseph reacted to the news with a mixture of affront and alarm.[1] Ready to look down on the Desmousseaux for being in the theatre, he was actually terrified at the prospect of having to earn his own living, giving up all hope of being the respected begetter of genius. A fearful domestic row ensued in which he resorted to a variety of abuse and threats—first that the girl was worthless, second that it would be Catherine Franck who would suffer the most (a point upon which she seemed reluctant to enlighten anyone) and finally that César might be driven to commit a *crime passionel*, such as the scandal-provoking Choiseul-Praslin had recently been demented enough to do. It is greatly to Franck's credit that he allowed himself to be unmoved by any of these obvious attempts to lure him back, and even more commendable that he agreed to pay off Nicolas-Joseph's outstanding debt of 11,000 francs before marrying.

Slipping out of the house quietly one day when the rest of the family was out walking, César took up temporary abode with Félicité and her mother and father. They went through a brief period of engagement (it was then French law that one could not marry without parental consent until reaching the age of twenty-five) and finally set the date for 22nd February 1848. The day was notable for more than Franck's wedding, for by a remarkable coincidence it also happened to be that on which the 1848 revolution first made itself felt. The so-called 'February days' began on the very morning the couple walked out of Notre-Dame-de-Lorette as man and wife, cries of 'À bas Guizot' ringing out and a long students' chorus menacingly treading its way from the Panthéon to the Madeleine. Fortunately neither party was harmed, and once the abortive struggle for freedom had ended Franck was given his first organ post at the church at which he had been married. His sympathies with Louis-

[1] His discovery of the match came with his noting of his son's dedication of the song 'L'Ange et l'Enfant' to Félicité.

Napoléon, expressed in the form of the songs 'Les Trois Exilés', quickly faded, however, and even the limited bloodshed of this earliest outbreak leading up to the *coup d'état* of 1851 proved too vile for his pure sensibility. He had emerged to maturity none the less, and a new phase was now awaiting him.

CHAPTER III

FRANCK'S acceptance of his lot as a minor Parisian organist was as characteristic of him as anything he had previously done. He made no anguished scenes, neither did he outwardly reveal the disappointment he must have felt at what he thought was the end of his composing career. On the contrary, he seemed so glad to be rid of the spectre of his avaricious father and so contented at what seemed the promise of a happy marriage that a second breakdown that was impending was easily staved off. De Rollot, his choirmaster at Notre-Dame-de-Lorette, was a man of the cloth whose real function was ecclesiastical. Nevertheless he was so interested in musical developments inside the Church that he frequently assisted Franck in giving performances of the masses of Mozart, Haydn and Cherubini, making full use of the rich voices of those professional opera-singers who seemed to comprise so large a part of the congregation. Gradually the young organist built up a circle of acquaintances within the professional world, and he even became associated with Cavaillé-Coll, who was to be the builder of the next organ he was to command at Saint-Jean-Saint-François-au-Marais near the end of 1851. This worthwhile promotion was brought about by the Abbé Dorcel, an interested cleric who had heard Franck play and was determined to have him at his new church. The superior quality of this second organ, and the contacts made through Cavaillé-Coll, were to be the means of sustaining the composer for the next twenty years, so that when he moved to the yet greater post at Sainte-Clotilde (the one he was to occupy for the rest of his life) it was to a somewhat better version of the same environment that he went.

By that time his interest had been firmly engaged in composing short pieces for these marvellous new instruments. Beforehand, however, he was persuaded by the entreaties of his family to have a serious try at opera, a course almost obligatory for anyone hoping to make his name as a creative musician. Perhaps it is worth mentioning that Franck was not a total stranger to this genre. As a student he had sketched out some music for a stage work called *Stradella*, modelled on the life of the early Neapolitan composer. This small-scale venture had been nothing more than an exercise, however, and Franck had not even possessed the rights to the libretto. In the event, what music was written was discarded in 1843 and the work was left unpublished. When it came to a question of satisfying the pride of his in-laws, however, Franck naturally had to put up a better showing. The libretto this time was one concocted by Royer and Vaëz, two very experienced hands who had made their reputation with the French versions of Rossini's *Otello* and Donizetti's *Lucia di Lammermoor*. Despite not being in the best of health at the point of embarking on the work (the composer was advised to spend a few weeks in Switzerland recuperating), Franck took their story, *Le Valet de Ferme*, to set to music. It was a bad mistake all round, since the plot was far weaker than those usually associated with these competent writers, the former of whom was destined to become Director of the Opéra some years later. A tale about a hired labourer who becomes embroiled in an affair with his employer's wife—all set in eighteenth-century Ireland—it seems dour enough just in outline. On examining the details it becomes obvious that the whole work was unstageable. It is full of typical *ficelles*, badly forced rhyming couplets and creaking *science des planches*. One is surprised that someone with Mme Desmousseaux's theatrical background should have encouraged such banality.

César himself was quite insensitive to literary quality, and apparently saw nothing ominous about the project. When he was well enough, around 1853, he settled down to one of his grinding sessions of hard work, having written down the main features a year or two earlier. On its completion it was sent to Liszt, who again showed his generosity by writing to Escudier and generally using all his considerable influence to have the work mounted at the Opéra. Some publicity hinted that it had been accepted for production during the 1856 season, but this was not so. It may have been refused because it was technically an *opéra-comique* (i.e. it contained spoken dialogue),[1] but one can hardly doubt that its

---

[1] Franck's recitatives have, however, since come to light, so that in fact it could have been mounted.

merits, once thoroughly examined, were found to be too few to justify acceptance. Even Royer, after his appointment, did not consent to its inclusion in the repertory, and rumour has it that his part in the writing of the libretto had been done while half-asleep. Gallois describes the entire enterprise as 'unspeakable', and even Franck must have finally concurred since, very much later, when approached by a publisher about it, he conceded that it was too bad to issue. It is accordingly best to regard *Le Valet de Ferme* as most critics have subsequently viewed *Hulda* (Franck's second major opera)—that is, as a product of the theatrical influence of the Desmousseaux family. In the former case it was almost certainly the composer's mother-in-law who was the driving force; in the latter Franck's own son Georges, who partook of certain Desmousseaux characteristics in his constant meddling with dramatic subjects.

With failure in the orchestra pit and the opera house to haunt him it is not surprising that Franck relapsed into a further spell of silence. Sensing security within the church's sanctum, he paid a good deal more attention to his duties there than he did to composing. Also he was glad to be free from the tedium of hourly teaching commitments spread all over the city. He did not completely renounce these, but preferred instead to combine them with visits farther afield, such as his trips to Orléans, where the Desmousseaux family had relatives by the name of Féréol and where Franck had made an impression on the Director of the Conservatoire. During the years following his marriage he made regular excursions to that city, receiving in return rather more handsome emoluments than he had been used to and even being asked to give occasional organ recitals. It is a pity that these latter show the composer in such a poor light, for they were made up of the customary trifles of the salon unsuitably transcribed for performance within a church or on an instrument with clerical associations. Not only was there no evidence that Franck was devoted to Bach or the other baroque masters at this stage, but he even seemed indifferent towards the sensible suggestion of Bertholet, the director, that he include in his programmes some of the music of neglected Orléans composers of the past. Here one can detect a distinct difference between Franck and, say, d'Indy, who would almost certainly have seized upon any opportunity to increase his knowledge of the lesser French heritage and to demonstrate his superior erudition in such matters. Still, Franck acquired sufficient money through his Orléans tours to set up a new apartment in Paris and to enjoy some of the fruits of affluence.

When he finally resumed his interest in composition it was principally with the organ in mind. With Cavaillé-Coll's invention (which the composer referred to innocently as resembling an orchestra) at his side it was only natural that he should eventually write a few pieces to show off its paces. Before he could do that, however, he had first of all to master the wealth of new resources, including couplers and a great variety of added stops, which were about to transform the instrument. He was rather slow to do this (not perhaps being as alive to their potentialities as his Belgian contemporary Lemmens, whose feats were beginning to be reported with lustre in the press), and apparently belonged more to that generation of French organists who had let the instrument run down both in repertoire and resources since the eighteenth century. The truth is that the French Revolution had had a particularly bad effect on the standing of the organ in France, not simply because so many fine specimens were destroyed during the fighting but also because the idea of organ-playing was replaced by the singing of patriotic hymns, march-tunes and other expressions of national feeling. Some composers, too, found more of interest in the concert-hall. Opera, it goes without saying, stole the greatest share of interest. However we look upon it, the period between the Revolution and, say, 1850 was an inglorious one as far as the French organ was concerned, François-Henri Clicquot (who died in 1790) being the last of the eighteenth-century exponents. It was to be part of Franck's function to help restore some of Clicquot's organs at about this time in his life, their restoration probably being intended as a sop to the church from a mock-contrite government. Many of them had been severely damaged, but even the well-preserved ones struck some listeners—Mendelssohn being a prime case—as sounding like a 'choir of old women'.

Surprisingly—and most people associate Franck first and foremost with the organ—the composer did not write prolifically for the instrument, as did one or two of his pupils like Tournemire and Vierne. He waited until he had obtained his Sainte-Clotilde post in 1858 before doing the serious practice necessary to conquer the new skills, and it was during the phase 1860–2 that he completed his *Six Pièces*—by common consent regarded as his first works of real importance. That these skills did not

* come to him quickly or confidently may be attributed to a number of factors. Though the work of restoration and the new appointment to Sainte-Clotilde may have swung Franck's thoughts in the direction of organ composition, it should be remembered that he was originally, in 1858, appointed *maître de chapelle*, with Théodore Dubois as organist, and transferred to the post of organist in the following year. Hence for the first year his time was spent in choir-training and refurbishing the vocal repertoire. He was not, however, a good choral conductor. He also found plainsong distasteful, and it puzzled and disappointed admirers of the composer as a church musician (as, for example, Charles Bordes in the 1880s) that he showed himself only too willing to skirt that category. What Franck really wanted was to cherish his beloved organ, with its three manuals and a very well-equipped pedal board. This he was permitted to do, and the repertoire he eventually sought was to be found more among Bach's fugues and fantasias than among the great choral works of the Renaissance.

Joseph Franck, who had meanwhile surprised César by taking first prize for organ at the Paris Conservatoire (where he had followed in his brother's footsteps), had written a set of six Preludes and Fugues for the instrument, adding the title of composer to his accomplishments and acting as a painful spur to César. The famous *Six Pièces*, which their composer gave not only at Sainte-Clotilde but also in November 1867 at Saint-Denis and again at the Trinity in 1869, were accordingly inspired as much by brotherly rivalry as by any firm desire to re-enter the lists as a creative artist. Their success, however, probably accounted for the spate of minor compositions that followed, including the *Cinq Petites Pièces pour Harmonium: Deux Offertoires, Deux Versets* and *Une Communion*. The year 1865 also saw the production of the rather better-known but no less trivial or defective *Les Plaintes d'une Poupée* for piano and *La Tour de Babel* for soloists, choir and orchestra. The little piano piece may well have been written, like Debussy's *La Boîte à Joujoux*, to please a child of the composer's, for by this time Franck had become a father several times over. His parental experience had been tragic (two of his four children dying in infancy), so he was probably all the more inclined to fuss over the survivors. Marie-Joseph (1849–50) and Paul (1856–9) were victims of common childhood diseases, but the first-born, Georges, whom his father nicknamed 'barricades' on account of his birth during the 'Year of Revolutions', and the younger, more obscure Germain, who ultimately pursued the unlikely career of Inspector of Railways (Bridges and Footpaths Division), were both palpable presences in the Franck apartment, now situated in the Boulevard St Michel and not, as originally, in the Boulevard Montparnasse. The fragile doll's lament should not be considered a major contribution to Franck's piano music. His great works for the piano (which Maurice Emmanuel claimed was more suited to him than the organ) were to emerge in the middle of the 1880s, and were almost comparable to those of Busoni in view of the paucity of substantial, contrapuntal virtuoso pieces in France at that time.

Little need be said about *La Tour de Babel*, except that like *Ruth* it gave the composer practice at oratorio without bringing him the slightest reward. Failing even to find a publisher, it remains to this day the least known of Franck's larger enterprises. Also, like *Ruth*, it was built on a biblical parable and somehow did not overcome a certain feebleness in its material. This was more reprehensible with such a rousing subject and in view of the composer's intervening experience. Probably its consignment to oblivion stemmed from the fact that Franck once more succumbed to the temptation to turn what could have been an intensely dramatic experience into a stuffy piece of sermonizing in the form of a dialogue between God and Man. Musically there is a case for saying that the work was no worse than many others Franck was to write later, but, as usual, he failed in the task of relating theme and music in the minds of his hearers. Most critics today regard the work as having provided the composer with the experience to write *Les Béatitudes* (there is a somewhat similar vocal antiphony in the styles of the two undertakings) and nothing more. Such a view is possibly the most charitable one to take, since if the listener is disinclined to mount a rescue operation for *Rédemption* and *Les Béatitudes* (and most are) he is not likely to go out of his way to save this earlier and on the whole less accomplished work from critical damnation. It is odd that, despite offering itself as a good choice for a musician in search of a text, this parable has never found a composer to do it justice. How many of his admirers, for example, are aware that Stravinsky made a setting of it in 1944? And, of these, how many can claim to have heard a performance of it?

The *Six Pièces*, on the other hand, can be heard on almost every week's programmes on one radio station or another. Deferring analysis of them to a later portion of the book, it is sufficient to state that the beautiful *Prélude, Fugue et Variation* (which was incidentally transcribed for piano by both Franck himself and the late Harold Bauer) deserves its place as one of the finest single organ pieces written since the days of Bach, as well as being important in establishing the tripartite form its composer was subsequently to use for other and better known keyboard works. In addition it posed the dialogue idea used extensively in the Piano Quintet (1879) and has a similar tonal structure to the finale of the *Variations Symphoniques*, upon which the composer worked at Azilles in the summer of 1885. The dedications of the *Six Pièces* are to Franck's organ-playing friends: Chauvet, Alkan, Saint-Saëns, Cavaillé-Coll, Benoist and Lefébure-Wély. Aside from the above-named triptych, they comprise a *Fantaisie* (also considered among the best of the set, and among the most often played), a *Grande Pièce Symphonique*, a *Pastorale*, *Prière* and *Final*. These latter do not merit quite such extravagant praise as, for instance, Léon Vallas bestows upon them. They hover uncertainly between unctuousness and bombast. But, regarded as a unified collection, they stand apart from Franck's previous work and remain a milestone in the progress of organ composition in France during the nineteenth century. Liszt went further than Vallas by openly comparing them with Bach when he visited Sainte-Clotilde to hear them for the first time. This testimonial in itself did Franck a great deal of good with his congregation and with the organ fraternity in Paris. It established him as a front-rank composer for the instrument.

The only remaining work of significance to have sprung from the early organ period was not instrumental, but a *Mass for three voices* which the composer began about 1859-60, though he was unable to finish it, at least to the specifications required for publication, until 1872. This undistinguished contribution to the genre rates as one of Franck's few genuinely liturgical compositions (as opposed to his more customary quasi-liturgical settings for which he unquestionably had a greater aptitude) and was in all likelihood brought into being by some clerical prodding on the part of his superiors. Yet the composer did seem to have a brief ecclesiastical phase around this period. His *Trois Motets* appeared under the auspices of Régnier-Canaux in 1858, as did the little-known *Messe Solennelle pour basse solo et orgue*, which may well have lit the spark for the later work. The *Mass for three voices* makes use of soprano, tenor and bass voices accompanied by an organ, harp, cello and double-bass. Among the sections are a Kyrie, Agnus Dei, Sanctus and Gloria, with Credo and Panis Angelicus added. A performance (in somewhat truncated form) actually took place at Sainte-Clotilde on the 2nd April 1861 under Franck's direction. It was not entirely private, the public being allowed admission for the sum of fifty centimes. Almost all the musicians who heard the work had something derogatory to say about it with the exception of Charles Bordes, who was later to develop reservations. D'Indy, when he saw the score, surprisingly described the syrupy cello sequences of the Gloria as unremittingly vulgar. 'La musique cathédralesque' was Saint-Saëns's less damaging but equally scornful response to it. One of Franck's most recent biographers, Maurice Kunel, has referred to this section as 'de son goût pompeux', while Emmanuel Buenzod claims confidently that Franck could have had no conception at this time of Renaissance splendour. Only the sentimental Panis Angelicus has won plaudits from the undiscriminating.

Of the several movements the work comprises, the Kyrie and Agnus Dei seem to have escaped with the least criticism. They were the earliest parts to have been written. The Credo, which is in sonata form, strikes a curiously German note and must have been the most arduous to write. Perhaps it is worth remarking that two drafts were made of the Agnus— rather an unusual procedure for a composer so lacking in self-criticism. The Gloria is undoubtedly the worst movement. Its use of the harp to express celestial emotions may have been relatively new when Franck employed it, but has since become the most glutinous of all orchestral effects. By comparison the *Messe Solennelle* has been designated as 'timidly respectable'—another piece of typical phraseology when it comes to describing the composer's church music as a whole. Besides these two large undertakings there were *Trois Offertoires*, dating from 1871 and consisting of *Quae est ista*, *Domine Deus in simplicitate* and *Dextera*

Domini. These were of no special importance and were probably composed merely in order to strengthen the musical archive of SainteClotilde. Franck had a habit of extending his offertories unconsciously, so perhaps it was a relief to the clergy that he took to writing them down in advance. Also written in pedestrian fashion for church use seem to have been two further vocal works, *Domine non secundum* for soprano, tenor and bass and *Quare fremuerunt gentes* for choir, three voices and organ with the favoured doublebass added. The latter appeared in the same year as the *Offertoires*. The following year, 1872, that which saw the addition of the Panis Angelicus, witnessed the composition of a brief hymn, *Veni Creator*, for tenor and bass, similar in dimensions to the earlier *Ave Maria* (1863), only omitting the soprano. All these specimens of *la musique sacrée* should be distinguished from the major oratorios or *scènes bibliques* of the period around the FrancoPrussian War when the composer was either about to be appointed or had been installed as Professor of Organ at the Conservatoire.

Actually the first of the huge frescoes to be completed was called neither an oratorio nor a biblical scene but a *poèmesymphonique*.[1] This was the composer's setting of Édouard Blau's *Rédemption*, for mezzosoprano, chorus and orchestra, which occupied him throughout the austere years 1871–2. The score that we know today differs considerably from the original. Like most of Franck's religious works it was a disaster in its first incarnation. The story recounts Man's progress from his primeval state of ignorance and later degeneracy towards the acceptance of religious belief. The division of the score into two parts, separated by an orchestral interlude, did not result in avoidance of monotony. Blau's treatment of the paganism of Part I was mild and lethargic, and Franck matched this with equally unterrifying music. An archangel enters near the end of this section announcing the coming of Christ, and the section concludes with a depressingly flat chorus celebrating his birth. Whatever merits it has, Part I is notable mainly for its tonal adventurousness. The interlude (which was originally omitted in the performance given by Colonne at the Odéon Theatre in Holy Week, 1873, owing to lack of rehearsal time

[1] It is worth mentioning this since Franck commenced work on *Les Béatitudes* in 1869, allegedly completing the Prologue and the first two beatitudes before moving on to *Rédemption*.

and poor copying of the parts) was not much better. The proclaiming of humanity regenerate in Part II was the most successful episode, but even this was mishandled at the première. A year or so later Franck reissued the work with cuts in the subtitles, changes into more amenable keys and some recasting of the interlude, and in this form it had a second performance in March 1875.

Les Béatitudes, the other post-war epic, took Franck till 1879 to complete, though he had been meddling with it since the year before the conflict. In effect it is a series of texts from the Sermon on the Mount, suitably arranged in poetic sequence by a Mme Colomb, wife of a teacher at a Versailles lycée. A prologue precedes the eight Beatitudes, each of which attempts to convey some biblical tenet. A formidable work in scope and size, it can only be called an oratorio and has indeed been compared to such great and diverse compositions as Bach's B minor Mass, Brahms's Requiem and Wagner's *Parsifal.* By any account it was considered by Franck himself to be of the utmost importance among his works, and despite his ultimate reputation as a chamber musician it is probable that he continued to the day of his death to regard it as his mightiest single work. Its thinned-down première at his apartment on the 20th February 1879 was the nadir of the composer's fortunes, the audience trooping out one by one until a few friends were left. The uncut version was not performed until after his death.

CHAPTER IV

LAUREATESHIP AT THE CONSERVATOIRE

HISTORIANS need not be reminded of the subtle changes wrought upon the nation's cultural life by the Franco-Prussian War and its bloody aftermath, the Commune. These events—the former arising out of a quarrel over the Hohenzollern claim and the latter out of much the same sentiments as had already expressed themselves unsuccessfully in 1789 and 1848—turned the nation on its head to such an extent that its military and religious principles were severely shaken and even its traditional art-forms brought into question. Its great literary and musical heroes of pre-war years—men like Hugo, Lamartine, Meyerbeer and the belatedly admired Berlioz—had, by the time things returned to normal, been pushed aside or reached the end of their pilgrimage. New names were being touted with the old chatter and fervour, some of them reformers and others merely the exponents of a new naturalism that was to form the basis of the modern movement. They all made the strutting figures of the Second Empire look like pasteboard cavaliers. Zola, with his brutally realistic novels and his ultimate championship of the Dreyfus cause, was a clear example of the type of artist to be engendered by the Third Republic. Maupassant, his more cynical counterpart, was another. The Impressionist movement in painting, led by Manet, Pissarro, Monet, Sisley and others, brought fresh optical vigour to replace the outworn Romanticism of Delacroix or Courbet's quieter fidelity to events. In music, which lagged a little behind the other arts, the appearance of the Société Nationale—of which both Franck and Saint-Saëns were founder members—betokened the flow or unexpected sequence of French chamber works and the diversion of taste from the ever-present opera-house to the concert-hall or recital room. Pasdeloup's *Jeunes Artistes* made Sunday orchestral concerts vehicles for a new breed of composer, as did the Wagnerian-based *Concerts Colonne* and *Nouveaux Concerts* promoted by Lamoureux. The age of music and diamonds was over and something more closely resembling Sir Henry Wood's Promenade venture was at hand to take its place.

That this change was of immense material benefit to Franck is obvious. It catapulted him right into the centre of musical activity and gave him the certainty that his works would be played and discussed. The first stroke of luck to come his way after the rioting had died down was his appointment as Professor of Organ in succession to his old teacher, Benoist, at the Conservatoire. To this day it remains a minor mystery how Franck was able to pluck such a choice plum from the academic tree. Some say it was his former choirmaster, Théodore Dubois, who put in a good word for him with Ambroise Thomas, at that time the institution's director. Others have argued that Saint-Saëns (who would himself have made an excellent candidate had his composing and general intellectual interests not taken up all his time) went around canvassing for Franck. On the face of it this latter supposition seems unlikely in view of the two men's well-known animosity over so many matters. At any rate d'Indy—who incidentally became one of the first of the new professor's official pupils—passes over the incident in his biography as being mildly incomprehensible. Perhaps, for once, French musicians showed an element of fair dealing, for there can be no possible doubt that, among all the contenders, Franck was easily the best qualified man for the job. Unfortunately he too had ambitions as a composer, and these finally took precedence over instrumental teaching with frequently embarrassing results.

Of course the actual appointment had to come through the official channels—in this case through the gift of the Ministre des Beaux-Arts, a M. Jules Simon. But he acted on Thomas's recommendations without evident demur. The salary fixed was quite princely by Franck's standards (1,500 francs rising to 2,400 francs per annum) though not as high as that paid to the various professors of composition, of whom Massenet was the chief but also including Massé, Reber and Bazin. Not without reason Franck hoped that he would eventually be promoted to one of these posts, but as they fell vacant they were filled by others, notably by Guiraud (Debussy's teacher) and Delibes. Franck's ideas on composition were not kindly regarded by the director, and when it was discovered that he used his organ classes to pass on the creative urge a distinctly frosty attitude was taken up towards him. Yet Franck had never been a man to bemoan the loss of small dues. He felt happy and secure at the Conservatoire, despite all backbiting, and quickly settled down to eighteen years of fruitful labour which, in the event, were to prove the finest years of his composing career and a period of incalculable in- fluence on his art.

Aside from the continuous work he put in on *Les Béatitudes*, the first of the creations of Franck's Conservatoire phase was a splendid augury. Named *Les Éolides*, it was a second symphonic poem (allowing for the present that *Rédemption* had more the character of a cantata) and a most accomplished essay. Written in 1876—though possibly sketched a few months earlier—it attempts to portray the *brises flottantes* of Leconte de Lisle's poem about a classical race of pixies called the Aeolids.[1] Not being of a very literary turn (though the composer did pen a few more *mélodies*, such as *Roses et Papillons* and the famous *Nocturne*, in the 1870s and 80s), Franck had to wait upon an additional source of inspiration for this important work, which looks forward as none of his others do to the Impressionist landscapes of Debussy. This extra dimension came in the form of a brief holiday he spent at the home of his friend Auguste Sanches at Azilles in the province of Languedoc. It was while on his way to this retreat that the composer encountered the mistral at Valence, and the experience is said to have jogged his mind in the direction of de Lisle's verses. The composition was a surprise to his Parisian friends, some of whom might have dissuaded him had they had the opportunity, but fortunately it was presented more or less as a *fait accompli* at the Salle Érard in November 1876. This was probably what sparked off the series of symphonic poems for which Franck is so well known, though it was to be a further six years before the appearance of *Le Chasseur Maudit*, eight before *Les Djinns* and almost the end of his life before *Psyché*, the work with which *Les Éolides* has most in common. Together these outpourings present us with a new Franck, less solemn and more animated; many still regard it as a pity that he did not follow the course set by them more conscientiously. They are not exactly conventional symphonic poems (voices appear in *Psyché* and a piano *obbligato* in *Les Djinns*), but they

[1] De Lisle, though not widely read today, was notable for having also in- spired vocal works from Duparc, Fauré and several other contemporaries.

almost certainly inspired brilliant works in a similar vein from Chausson, Ropartz, Dukas and others among the circle.

As always d'Indy reminds us with some sharpness that Franck was really a composer of classical cast whose first instrument had been the piano. Thus he is able to press his analogies with the late Beethoven sonatas when he comes to discuss the two monumental triptychs. These were, respectively, the *Prélude, Choral et Fugue* (1885) and the less often heard *Prélude, Aria et Final* (1888). The dates refer to their premières, which were given by Mlle Marie Poitevin and Mme Bordes-Pène, the charming sister-in-law of Franck's pupil Charles Bordes. Both were to meet with misfortune, he dying of heart trouble in his forties and she suffering a paralysis which killed off her promising career as a pianist. The two works are not unlike—each is fugal and heavy with part-writing—but the earlier seems more inspired and has certainly caught the imagination of players to a greater degree. Why did Franck return to write these epic solo works for the piano after having virtually abandoned the instrument for nearly twenty years? D'Indy tells us that the composer was irritated by the run-down condition of the repertory, and it seems that he did once say something of the kind to his still devoted followers. Yet it is hard to believe that this was his real motive. After all, there had been superb works for piano written since Beethoven. Discounting the marvellous sonatas Schubert wrote in the last few weeks of his life, which it really took Schnabel to resurrect in the 1920s and 30s, one may still point with pride to the impressive works of Schumann and Chopin, while Franck would have had to be disingenuous to deny that much of his pianism had been learned from Liszt. The B minor opening of the *Prélude, Choral et Fugue* certainly recalls the mood (as it does the key) of Liszt's grand Sonata. D'Indy's protestations are too transparent to accept in full. Part of Franck's intention surely stemmed from his original training as a virtuoso (now given a fresh and slightly different opportunity to display itself) and partly from the connection of the piano with the chamber ensemble for which he had written in 1879. His Piano Quintet, whatever we may think of its erotic tone, was a tremendous success in one of the most difficult genres. The writing of it must have put the composer in mind of keyboard figuration again.

One is inclined to accept this last explanation in view of the added return to the organ which had immediately preceded the Quintet. Asked for *Trois Pièces*, by which to celebrate Guilmant's inauguration of the Trocadéro organ, Franck complied with another *Fantaisie*, a *Cantabile* and a *Pièce Héroique*. None of these commissioned works strikes a profound note, and they are not generally as good as the *Six Pièces* of the early 1860s. Nevertheless they rearoused interest in instrumental composition, and were perhaps a reaction against the seemingly endless work put in on *Les Béatitudes*. It is very hard to say whether Franck's organ works exceed his piano works in merit. The balance seems about the same as in the executant sphere. One thing is indisputable. The *Trois Pièces* are not nearly as good as the three plain *Chorals* the composer was to jot down (paradoxically on an old piano) at Nemours in the last year of his life. These serene masterpieces look forward to the best organ works of Alain, Tournemire and Duruflé in a way that the middle set most assuredly do not.[1] They, on the contrary, remain products of the age of the symphonic organ and quite lack Franck's intense and solitary spirituality. However, they served their purpose (Guilmant, despite surviving to help found the Schola Cantorum, was essentially a nineteenthcentury player), and if they also assisted Franck in directing his thoughts to the smaller forms they should be applauded for that alone, for not only did *Les Béatitudes* come to grief but so did the composer's last two operas, *Hulda* and *Ghisèle*. His works with keyboard (the Violin Sonata and the *Variations Symphoniques* are ready examples) were on the contrary among his supreme successes. The whole question of organ versus piano is problematic in Franck's output. Everyone knows that the organ world is an enclosed one—many musicians never enter it either as players or listeners. On the other hand the piano is possibly, as Sidney Harrison insists, 'the best instrument of all'. This being so, it is inevitable that Franck's organ works are appreciated only by the few, while his piano works are often ignorantly said to reflect organ textures. In fact they do (as they also reflect Franck's enormous stretch), but not always or necessarily to their detriment.

To appreciate Franck at his best one has to immerse oneself in the

[1] To savour these magnificent works to their utmost it is necessary to hear the recording made of them by the late Jeanne Demessieux shortly before her premature death from cancer in 1969.

chamber works. The Quintet, as we have said, is a deeply sublimated work, allegedly inspired by the composer's illicit passion for Augusta Holmès, one of his later pupils. It has its faults—including a too-quick reversion to the opening F minor after having switched to A minor for the second movement—but its *dolcissimo ma cantabile* is sublime, and its finale brilliantly despondent. Much finer and more interestingly constructed is the evergreen Violin Sonata (1886), said to have been promised to Cosima von Bülow but in fact dedicated, many years later, to Eugène Ysaÿe and bestowed on him as a wedding present. Franck wrote nothing greater than this alternately erudite and melodious work with its four deeply contrasting movements. The opening chord on the piano, followed by the violin's ascending and descending arpeggio, with the whole repeated in sequence, has come to be indissolubly associated with the bird-song in Proust's famous novel in which a similar sonata is composed by a fictional musician by the name of Vinteuil. Commentators are still much divided over whether or not Franck was the model for Vinteuil and whether his sonata was the origin of the one in which the notorious 'little phrase' occurs. Most accept the assumption, but George Painter—the novelist's chief biographer—tends to favour a composite portrait in which the sonata is identified variously—at one point Franck's, at another Saint-Saëns's D minor and at yet another the first of Fauré's two examples of the form. It seems incredible that Saint-Saëns, with his early success and choleric disposition, could have acted as the model for Vinteuil, though Fauré offers himself as a more acceptable possibility. Neither, however, spent his early adulthood in a French provincial town, unless we make an exception for the very brief period during which Fauré was an organist at Rennes. As Proust was passionately fond of music of all kinds, including the modern works being written by Debussy, it seems unlikely that we shall have a definitive solution to this problem.[1]

The special features which commend Franck's sonata over those of, say, Brahms are easy enough to make clear. Aside from the four-movement form Franck employs a long *recitativo quasi-fantasia* in his third movement which proclaims his fondness for Bach's unaccompanied

[1] See *Marcel Proust,* 2 vols., by George Painter (Chatto & Windus, 1965).

works. He also offers the listener one of the most perfect specimens of canon in the opening of the finale.[1] Despite some glorious *cantilena* for the violin in the *Allegretto*, it is apparent from the *étude*-like nature of the piano writing in the second movement which is Franck's real instrument. It exemplifies all he had learnt from Chopin and Liszt. Otherwise Brahms is possibly the only serious contender Franck has in this genre, the 'Regenlied' movement of his G major Sonata, Op. 76, and the whole of the huge D minor, Op. 108, being respectively beguiling and stirring. Franck's composition had its public première in Brussels with Ysaÿe on the violin and Mme Bordes-Pène at the piano. It almost resulted in disaster, since it took so long to play that the light by which to read the music became unfavourable. Ysaÿe, with customary ebullience, tapped the music-stand with his bow and called out 'Allons!'—a signal for both partners to race through the remainder of the work from memory. It is interesting that Franck originally intended the opening movement to be played quite slowly, but on hearing Ysaÿe decided to mark it *Allegretto*. So many legends surround the work that it is difficult to retell them all. Ysaÿe and Pugno carried it around the world as a rallying point for French culture, and its popularity did so much for that nation's chamber music that it is tempting to ascribe most of the revivals associated with Debussy and Ravel to it. Certainly Chausson's *Poème* of ten years later must have owed something to it, for we are shown yet again in literature a portrait of the last-named composer playing the sonata with Ysaÿe in Rodin's studio. The portrait occurs in Camille Mauclair's novel about Paris, *The City of Light*.[2]

Franck's last and possibly supreme chamber work was the String Quartet of 1889. It is surprising, with his adoration of Beethoven, that he had not begun one before. But it is evident from d'Indy's description

[1] I once heard Sviatoslav Richter plunge into this flowing canon too quickly for his partner, David Oistrakh, with the result that they were compelled to start again. The performance, however, was unforgettable for other reasons.

[2] Reverberations from this sonata even found their way into sculpture according to many authorities. Victor Rousseau's statue *Ecstasy* was widely assumed to have been hewn on hearing it. Its nakedness is at odds with the purity of the music, but the sentiments aroused by it are not altogether at variance with Franck's earlier music, especially the Quintet.

of the hallowed atmosphere that surrounded the venture that this was probably because the composer had considered himself too ignominious to attempt such a climb. There is no doubt that he had a hard time writing it; the first movement alone took him from spring to autumn of the year in question. By comparison he finished the *Scherzo* in a mere ten days. His favourite movement, however, was to be the *Larghetto*, a stream of melody that so thrilled him that he had to call in his pupil and exclaim wildly: 'I have got it at last. It is a most beautiful phrase!' Taken as a whole the Quartet is as complex in form as any of the later Beethoven works, commencing with a dual structure described by d'Indy as 'sonata form within a *lied*'. The modulations are unusual too, involving excursions into keys only distantly related to the tonic. This first movement is indeed very large and almost dwarfs the remainder when we consider that at least one of its themes—the one described as the *lied*—recurs in the finale in the cyclical fashion Franck utilized for so many of his late works. The Quartet is perhaps unique in the composer's work in having been vociferously acclaimed at first hearing. This was in April 1890, only a few months before his death. 'At last people are beginning to understand me!' exclaimed Franck in rapture. Certainly he had good cause to feel that this was so, since the première was followed quite soon by a revival at Tournai. Yet Franck is not really known through this intimate and moving composition any more than is Fauré through the exceedingly beautiful Quartet he left on his death in 1924. Each seems to speak of 'last things', and for this reason does not make much impact on the young. If we had to find a word to describe them it would be 'resignation'—that sensation that everything has been experienced, lived through and gradually cast aside in favour of denial of the self. With the exception of *Les Béatitudes* Franck probably thought it his best work.

As the reader will have gathered, during the years when the composer was writing these gentle masterpieces for the new media, encouraged by the Société Nationale, he was also drawing acclaim as a teacher and as a figurehead around which the society's activities increasingly revolved. By the middle of the 1880s (when Franck's stipend had reached his maximum, after spending twelve years as professor) moves were made by his grateful pupils to secure honours for him. Franck himself characteristically never took a single step in the direction of canvassing for greater

prestige. Yet d'Indy and the others were tireless in pursuing government ministers and others in whose power these things lay. Albert
Cahen, brother of Count Louis Cahen d'Anvers and friend of Guy de
Maupassant, was the most successful in his scheme to brief the portrait-
painter Léon Bonnat to hint to the President that Franck was a deserving
candidate. The prize-giving day at the Conservatoire for 1885 consequently saw Franck wearing the ribbon of a Chevalier of the Legion
of Honour. The citation mentioned his services to organ-teaching, but
curiously omitted reference to his compositions. This led several of the
more pugnacious disciples to suspect—possibly rightly—that the award
was merely the customary 'handshake' offered to all long-serving professors and in no way reflected the diverse and formidable efforts the
composer had put into improving French music. He himself was again
unduly modest, as he was after the concert given later in his honour
(*see* page 41). It is possible that he was sincere, for he appeared more
touched by the four hundred cards of greeting he received—all assuring
him that he had supporters and well-wishers around him for the first
time in his life. Possibly, too, he had been more pleased with the laurel
wreath with which the Conservatoire itself had presented him five years
previously to commemorate his examination successes. In the meantime
he had been elected an Officier de l'Académie, so that in his last decade
he could hardly be said to lack distinction in the purely worldly sense.

An acrimonious kind of success also came to him through the feuding
at the Société Nationale. This body, whose original motto had been *Ars
Gallica* and which had been devoted to the promotion of native music,
had in recent years been increasingly involved with the cult of Wagner—
a cult Franck himself took little interest in but which intrigued pupils
like d'Indy, Duparc and Chausson. These men consequently proposed
opening the doors of the society a little wider so as to admit foreign
works of distinction.[1] They knew this would bitterly antagonize the
president, Saint-Saëns, who had a nervous phobia about German music
and had never forgiven Wagner for his playlet, *Eine Kapitulation*, written
at the time of the Franco-Prussian War. Correct in their assumptions,
they only had to wait for the full spleen of their leader to reach its pre-

[1] It should be recalled that Wagner was still taboo in France at this time. It
was 1887 before *Lohengrin* was performed at the Eden Theatre.

dicted level for him to stalk out, resignation in hand. This was precisely what happened, and d'Indy cleverly contrived to steer Franck into his chair as the slightly bewildered advocate of a change of policy. In time, of course, the power-driven composer of the *Symphonie Cévénole* knew perfectly well that he would inherit the office. He showed the patience to wait, and was duly rewarded on Franck's death in 1890. For five brief years, however, the composer enjoyed the immense privilege of heading the country's principal musical association. Perhaps it was this sort of elevation that led his adversaries to suspect him of being more devious than he appeared, and it also led cynics like Bordes to claim that the old man was nothing more than an invention of his pupils. The truth surely lies between these extremes.

The final tribute to the composer came on 30th January 1887, when the circle organized a festival of his works at the Cirque d'Hiver. Unhappily this was one of those occasions when the recipient of the honour was surprisingly dishonoured. It was not entirely his fault. The programme was compiled in two parts. Part I was conducted by Pasdeloup, now a very aged and unreliable conductor, and was to consist of *Le Chasseur Maudit*, the *Variations Symphoniques* and an extract from *Ruth*. In the second half, in which Franck himself was asked to take up the baton, the *Marche* and *Air de Ballet* from the opera *Hulda* were to be combined with the Third and Eighth Beatitudes. As usual the orchestra was badly rehearsed and a genuine débâcle occurred in the *Variations Symphoniques*, when Pasdeloup's vague beat caused the first violins to come in a shade before the piano. After a few bars they got hopelessly out of touch, as Sir Thomas Beecham would have said. Franck's own performance was only marginally better in that he did not make any crashing errors. Even so the two Beatitudes sounded poorly because of their remote tonality, involving the musicians in some nightmarish sight-reading. The outcome was therefore far from what the organizers wanted, and Franck's reputation once more began to decline. Fortunately the Quartet was yet to come—along with the less immediately successful Symphony. Franck's taste of glory was inevitably very brief, then, and in many respects he was one of those composers whose posthumous acclaim tends to outshine their lifework. At any rate, it was with an element of contrition, if not guilt, that critics eventually hoisted him on to the pedestal of fame while his body rested in the Montrouge cemetery—a not untypical example of a prophet being honoured too little and too late by the mediocrities who had joined to attack his every move while alive. *De mortuis nil nisi bonum.* . . .

CHAPTER V

DEATH AND INHERITANCE

BEFORE Franck's untimely death at the age of sixty-eight, however, he still had works to complete. Even as late as 1880–1 he had still been endeavouring to perpetuate his biblical scene-painting with the cantata *Rébecca*, of which only the camel-drivers' chorus won successive hearings. This was to be the last of his overtly religious works, and if it did not prove to him that he was a failure in this sphere it at least suggested as much. Like *Ruth* (the style of which it emulates) it was cut up into sec-tions—five this time—and survived in dismembered form. It did not compare with the series of tone-poems which the composer was dis-couraged from continuing. Part of the disapproval sprang from within the family. Georges—now a university lecturer and amateur anthropolo-gist—insisted time and again that his father re-enter the operatic arena. In this request he was supported by his mother, who was beginning to feel she had married a nonentity and was getting tired of scraping along on what she regarded as a miserable pittance. It is easy to blame these long-suffering people. The fact was, however, that Franck's superior, Massenet, to take one striking example, was earning the equivalent of £25,000 per year through his operas, *Manon* in particular having brought him in a fortune.[1] In theory it all seemed too easy. Franck should simply choose a better subject and *ipso facto* he could be a rich man within the year. Unfortunately Georges was as inept as his grandfather Nicolas-Joseph when it came to stage-managing the composer's career. One would have supposed him capable of lighting on a more promising subject than *Hulda*, but it was not to be. Franck accordingly ploughed through the task of completing eight hundred pages of score chiefly in order to placate his relatives—a labour that lasted from 1881, the date at which he finished *Rébecca*, to 1886, that on which he put the last note to the Violin Sonata.

[1] See James Harding's *Massenet* (Dent, 1970) for a delightful account of the career of this 'crafty old fox', as Rimsky-Korsakov labelled him.

Franck

The plot of *Hulda* is almost as ridiculous as that of *Le Valet de Ferme*. This time, however, it was a good deal more bloodthirsty. Quite likely it was modelled on the more horrific works of Meyerbeer which no one had the wit to see had gone out of fashion with the demise of the Empire. It was Massenet's daring love scenes that drew the crowds, and Franck was as incapable of this sort of sweetness as he was of that swashbuckling form of heroics created by his Berlin-born predecessor. *Hulda* originated in a play by Björnson about the eleventh-century Norwegians—in particular the tribe of Aslaks. Before being cast in operatic shape, however, it was first of all transformed into an idiotic melodrama by its librettist, Grandmougin. The name Hulda is that of the heroine, who is threatened successively by Gudleik (an Aslak warrior), Eiolf (the chieftain of a neighbouring tribe) and finally by what appears to be the whole race of captors under whose orders she is compelled to live. Each of these figures meets with a gory death in the course of the opera, as does Hulda herself, who commits a Tosca-like suicide at the final curtain. Predictably the director of the Opéra turned the work down flat. He was, however, impressed with the ballet of Winter and Spring which was placed at the beginning of the fourth Act (a virtually obligatory business in France, as the story of the première of *Tannhäuser* confirms). It was tactfully suggested to Franck that if he were to abstract the ballet it might go well on its own. This was too much for even his apologetic demeanour, and he abandoned the whole project without remorse or remonstrance. As it stands, the *Marche Royale* is probably the best set piece in *Hulda* which Georges managed to get performed in 1894 and 1895 but which drew only a few kind remarks from the faithful Tiersot.[1]

The last of all Franck's operas (neither he nor his family ever gave up trying) was the equally tendentious *Ghisèle*, where the action takes place in the Merovingian court of Neustria. The librettist for this work was Augustin-Thierry, a far better writer than Grandmougin. Again, it was performed posthumously, this time at Monaco in 1896, after the orchestration had been completed by several of the composer's pupils. The 'grand opera' style was once more a liability, and no further per-

[1] These were in the nature of an excuse, stating that the work was lyrical rather than dramatic and pointing to certain adequate sections, like the sword-song and prisoners' chorus, as providing a justification.

Death and Inheritance

formances followed, much to the disgust of Georges and his fellow labourers. It will be evident that Franck had not the slightest aptitude for opera, and would have done much better to have avoided the form. His perseverance with it reflects not simply family pressures but the long-standing influence of a debased tradition and even possibly the early friendship with Gounod, by now shattered. His inability to succeed with opera was basically due to his sheltered and undramatic personality. Such an explanation is reinforced if one reflects that he was writing *Ghisèle* at the same time in 1889 as he was working on the first movement of the Quartet. Could there be two compositions more utterly unlike? Sadly there is no record of any Franck pupil winning a triumph for himself in this popular genre. Almost all tried and failed in much the same manner as Franck himself. Duparc burnt his opera *Roussalka*; de Bréville had his *Eros Vainqueur* banned by the censor; Ropartz bored audiences with his austere *Le Pays*; and Lazzari actually drove them to ask questions in the Chamber of Deputies with his scarifying *La Lépreuse*. Bordes died whilst in the process of writing what looked as though it might turn out the best of them, the ill-fated *Les Trois Vagues*. Only d'Indy, whose *L'Étranger* was highly praised by Debussy, offers himself as a possible subject for a revival.

Franck's remaining works were few but infinitely more important. We have mentioned briefly the *Variations Symphoniques*, which set a valuable precedent by combining two forms—the concerto and the variation. This habit of harnessing together two previously independent conceptions is distinctively Franckian. We discover it as early as the *Prélude, Fugue et Variation* from the *Six Pièces*, and as late as the symphonic poem *Psyché* which almost partakes of the shape of a cantata. Outside of the solo piano pieces the *Variations* (first played by Louis Diémer as a reward for having performed the *obbligato* piano part in *Les Djinns*) offer the most convincing proof of Franck's ability to write well for the smaller keyboard instrument. They scintillate as much as a Chopin waltz, yet are as full of rich, muddy chords as an idiomatic Brahms slow movement. Contrast is so much in evidence in this work that one can understand why so many regard it as the composer's best. It effectively disperses his chief fault—the tendency to plod on monotonously with the same cluster of notes in a tempo that is neither fast nor slow. The

45

invention of a 'double theme' for varying is another instance of the work's unique ingenuity. Links with *Les Djinns* become evident in Variation VI, which is essentially an expressive reverie existing almost on its own. Incidentally, despite this numinous intrusion, no one can accuse the *Variations* of lacking spirit and volatility. They gave the lie to the commonly held view that Franck was only an 'organ-loft' composer, seriously deficient in a sense of gaiety. Probably no other piano work of the period has such a bouncing finale (subtly rhythmical as a result of its crossed accents), while the third variation has some of the most skimming piano figuration outside the pages of Litolff and Saint-Saëns. An arrangement has been made for piano solo, but it scarcely follows the intricacies of the original.

One of the other major enterprises upon which Franck embarked in this last, amazingly fruitful, decade was the final symphonic poem *Psyché*. Taken from an old fable by Sicard and de Fourcaud, the story was presented in three parts. It is the familiar tale of a girl who falls in love with Eros and is carried away to his abode amid a series of gentle but sensuous portents. It was a very daring theme to have chosen, though considering that Debussy was to set his *Bilitis* songs to verses by the lascivious Pierre Louÿs, it should not have seemed too outrageous in the *fin-de-siècle*. Indeed, in all probability Franck himself regarded the fable as harmless, and it was only the suspicious-minded who thought otherwise. Possibly some of the composer's friends, including the ubiquitous d'Indy, felt it necessary to defend him from an attack which was not worth answering, thus giving greater grounds for suspicion. True, Franck was still very much enamoured of Augusta Holmès (who had allegedly inspired the eroticism of the Quintet), and Mme Franck was distinctly shrewish in her whole attitude to such subjects. But it is quite tenable that Gustave Derepas, Gaston Poulin and others were correct in their assumption that the work was really a kind of Christian treatment of the Greek theme in which Eros is only a post-Platonic figure and the love which is celebrated more an asexual affair. The sections begin, first of all, with *Le Sommeil de Psyché*, in which the idealistic heroine is presented amid a cluster of dreams. Later in this section she is transported by creatures not unlike Franck's Aeolids in a peroration called *Psyché enlevée par les Zéphyrs*. Then follows a scene in *Les Jardins d'Éros* in which

Death and Inheritance

Franck's orchestration for the first time takes on a floating, Tristanesque quality, and its sequel, *Le Châtiment*, implying previous misdeeds. Finally the music moves on to *Les Souffrances et les plaintes de Psyché* (who is temporarily separated from her lover in Franck's score, but permanently so in the original myth) and the closing *L'Apothéose*. There is no doubt, whatever interpretation we care to place on it, that *Psyché* is a somewhat voluptuous work, full of a mysterious sense of levitation. It is hardly surprising to learn that Mme Franck mislaid her ticket to the première, held under the auspices of the Société Nationale on 10th March 1888.

Though she was almost entirely estranged from him at this time it is reasonable to suppose that Franck's wife was better pleased with the Symphony in D minor which made its appearance in 1889. Dedicated to his favourite Duparc, the work is a monument to sonority and quite eclipses the unsuccessful attempts at symphonic music made in France by men like Gossec, Lalo, Saint-Saëns, Bizet and even d'Indy. In its scope and aim it has much more in common with the works by Chausson, Magnard, Dukas and Roussel which it was to influence. Some critics have likened it to Liszt—citing *Les Préludes* as possessing a similar sound—but it is really more of the domain of Brahms or Wagner, perhaps the former rather than the latter, for it retains most of the classical gambits. These were modified in such a way as to anger the Parisian public none the less. In three movements instead of four, the work combines *Allegretto* and *Scherzo* in a particularly ingenious fashion. It is in this second movement that the cor anglais solo occurs—a conceit that provoked a severe response from one of the professors at the Conservatoire. Its combination with *pizzicato* strings, however, is irresistible, and if played at a good pace must continually delight. The first movement has a grave opening and only gradually gets away to its *Allegro*. The blazing brass 'Faith' theme, from among the second group, has again precipitated typical criticisms—that it polarizes around a weak mediant and generally fails in lyricism. Debussy, nevertheless, was agreeably surprised, his normally harsh comments being confined to the work's structure. The range of critical reaction was exceedingly wide. Poujaud agreed with Franck, echoing: 'Quelle belle sonorité! Et quel accueil.' The hostile Camille Bellaigue, however, gave the sternest rebuke in saying: 'Oh! l'aride et grise musique, dépourvue de grâce, de charme et de sourire!' Gounod was reputed to have rivalled this charge with his remark that the work was 'the affirmation of incompetence pushed to dogmatic lengths'. And Ambroise Thomas, the Conservatoire's director, is alleged to have maintained a stony silence. Hence Franck's symphony—now at the top of many popularity polls in Britain and the U.S.A.—had something less than an auspicious beginning.

The last actual compositions to flow from Franck's pen were the *Chorals* we have already mentioned, an admirable conclusion to a chequered career. Though, as we have said, they were sketched in Nemours, the registration was added on his return to Paris, and he was on the point of dedicating them when he entered his fatal illness. Legend has it that Augusta Holmès was again to be among the dedicatees, but in deference to the composer's widow his pupils recast the names so as to exclude her. Of the three numbers the last has always been the most popular with organists, though I have generally preferred the beautiful and ornamental set of variations based on the E major theme of No. 1. In a sense all three are concerned with the variation idea, and to that extent acted as a catalyst for organ works of a kind similar to the late Beethoven keyboard works for the piano repertory. They are written for grand organ, as were the Trocadéro pieces, but what is so inspiring about them is that they studiously avoid the rhetorical gestures normally associated with that ambiguous instrument. Remarkable as much as anything for their astonishing power of part-writing and modulation, the *Chorals* deserve the highest place in Franck's organ canon. He had said, before writing them, that he wanted to do something on the lines of Bach, and this time he came very close to succeeding. At least it is heartening to all the composer's admirers that he was able in the end to throw off the yoke of tame transcription or romantic imitation and write a sequence of works that sprang from much the same humble emotions as the baroque masterpieces. He was followed in the Chair of Organ by Widor—who might without injustice be described as the organist's Liszt—and several of his pupils were badly shaken by the virtuoso exercises they were made to do. But Franck's example in the *Chorals* left its own legacy, one which may be counted among the assets of such magnificent present-day players as Jean Langlais (now at Sainte-Clotilde, having followed

Gabriel Pierné, Tournemire and others), André Marchal and the late Marcel Dupré.

Franck's death, like Chausson's, was the result of an accident, though he lingered for several months. In May 1890 he was crossing the Pont Royal on his way to play the second piano part in a domestic performance of the *Variations Symphoniques* (using Paul Brand, the pianist of Ysaÿe's Quartet as soloist). Strolling along in a fit of absentmindedness he collided violently with the pole of a horseomnibus and was struck off his feet. People gathered around and suggested attention, but the composer hoisted himself up, brushed aside all protestations and continued on his way. He then spent a couple of exhausting hours practising, emerging from the evening's work in a bath of perspiration. As was his custom he walked back to the apartment at the Boulevard St Michel in the chilly night air. In retrospect his behaviour seems to have been signally illadvised, for despite his robust physique it became obvious that he had soon slid into a weakened state. Engagements were cancelled; he was unable to attend the revival of his Quartet, much to his distress; and in October he began to show symptoms of pleurisy. For three weeks he tossed and turned in bed, giving his doctors (the cousins Féréol from Orléans) and his immediate family cause for grave concern. Finally, on 7th November he had a relapse which presaged the end. Wrestling with some imaginary fugue subject, and every so often crying out 'Mes enfants, mes pauvres enfants!', he struggled through the night and died on the following day.[1] His funeral was held two days later and has presented biographers with a variety of malicious stories. These chiefly relate to the absence of so many eminent musicians from the graveside. D'Indy's absence is easily accounted for, since he was at Valence preparing for a concert. Possibly it was because he was given so little opportunity to return that he himself spread the ugly rumour that official musicians had combined to stay away. The truth is more complex. Certainly there was no representative from the Académie des BeauxArts, and Ambroise Thomas—from the Conservatoire—was missing. But he was an old man and the day a rainy one, and he can consequently be absolved from malice, especially as he felt an obligation to

[1] It is not clear whether this cry referred to his real or imagined family.

nominate a deputy to attend in his name. This turned out to be Delibes; but also present were Widor, who was to be Franck's successor, and a gathering of minor celebrities. From other institutions, or else privately, came Fauré, Bruneau, Cahen (who travelled from Belgium specifically to be there), Benoît, Guilmant, Joncières, Lalo and Augusta Holmès.

The major function—that of making the funeral address—oddly enough went to Chabrier, who was not a member of the circle and was relatively young (he was not yet fifty) to have been given such an honour. Possibly it was because Franck had always taken an unexpectedly paternal interest in him, having been the first to praise his *Douze Pièces Pittoresques* in 1880 and having consistently treated him with the seriousness he deserved. Chabrier, for all his buffoonery, was not slow to return the compliment. This time expressing himself with the utmost gravity he delivered a deeply moving oration which ran as follows:

> Farewell, master, and thank you, for you have done well! In you we salute one of the greatest artists of this century. We salute also the unrivalled teacher, whose wonderful instruction has produced a whole generation of musicians marked by energy, faith and serious intention, and armed at all points for strenuous battles which are often long contested. And finally the just and upright man, so humane and so disinterested, whose counsel was always sound and his words always kind. Farewell!

It is doubtful whether any of Franck's older associates could have conveyed so well the essence of his contribution to the art of music, the profession of teaching and the practice of morality. Chabrier was one of those exceedingly rare musicians—it is surprising in view of Berlioz and Debussy how many were French—who possessed the literary gift in almost equal measure. His associations with Verlaine and Théodore de Banville were perhaps what gave him this special quality, but even his casual letters as a clerk at the Ministry of the Interior are packed with apt descriptions and brilliant characterizations. The only eminent musician who seems genuinely to have deserted Franck's graveside was SaintSaëns, who had conveniently disappeared to Egypt a few days beforehand. Good manners were never SaintSaëns's strong point. In 1904 a more official gathering took place in the square of SainteClotilde to unveil Lenoir's monument to the composer.

Death and Inheritance

Briefly the attitude taken towards Franck in the years following his death may be said to have been excessively eulogistic in comparison with what he contended against in life. One cannot truthfully attribute this fact to the ultimate success of the String Quartet, much as one would like to. The truth is that oratorio was being belatedly recognized as a great form, and Franck's works in this form were being greeted with considerable acclaim in other countries—most notably of all, perhaps, by the country which had taken Handel into its bosom. Arthur Hervey's book, *French Music in the Nineteenth Century*, was published in Great Britain by the firm of Grant Richards in 1903, allowing just enough time for enthusiasts to have made a rough survey of the composer's achievements. Hervey was positively ecstatic in his praise of Franck, and his book devotes so many pages to the work of the pupils that he almost makes César seem the uncrowned king of French music, surpassing Gounod, Massenet and others who had made reputations for themselves in London. In 1906 one André de Ternant wrote a short satirical broadside in *The Choir*, mocking the reverence that had sprung up around the composer and incidentally implying that he had spent riotous years in Britain. This was quite deliberately inaccurate as Franck is never known to have visited this country.[1] His portrait as a comic hypocrite by de Ternant did not go down well here, neither was it kindly received by those of his countrymen who learned of it. Georges Servières, for example, was deeply indignant on Franck's behalf, having previously lauded the much-abused *Les Béatitudes* as 'a stream of exquisite melodies'. The critic of the *Débats*, too, must have had an attack of conscience, for Franck had not long been dead before he was writing in terms of a comparative study between this work and Bach's B minor Mass. His bold flights of praise had to be restrained by more senior figures.

One should remember also that it was only a mere two-score years after the composer's death that relations with Germany worsened again. This time there was no doubt as to where Franck's allegiances would have lain, and he was metaphorically disinterred as a reminder for patriots that France was preferred even by those with half-German ancestry if they had a grain of common sense. Since the composer had never made contact

[1] See Edward Lockspeiser's *Debussy—his Life and Mind*, Vol. I (Cassell, 1962).

with Wagner (the scapegoat on the other side as he was to be in World War II) it became easy to hold up Franck as the custodian of French musical values as opposed to many of his friends and pupils who had fallen under the spell of Bayreuth. Even Saint-Saëns, who had protested against foreign works being added to the Société Nationale repertoire, had unluckily been commended by Wagner before the rift; hence even he, the most chauvinistic musician in all France, did not seem quite ripe for canonization. D'Indy, too, though no one could have taken a more hysterical stand in the 1914–18 war, had earlier written a typically Wagnerian score in his *Fervaal* and had generally upheld the principles underlying the music-drama.[1] For a short while Franck was cast as the archetypal Frenchman, in fancy if not in fact. When the war was over—and the French public descended on Debussy and his friends like a plague of locusts—he was not long in being relegated to the second rank again.

Despite this posthumous demotion, from which he never entirely recovered, various attempts were made to elevate him by those who had grown tired of the *musicien maudit*. Cecil Gray pleaded his cause over here for a while and he was taken up by W. J. Turner. True, the composer was rudely attacked in Constant Lambert's *Music Ho!*, but Lambert's brilliantly erratic prophecies were not invariably a sound guide. The fact remained that concert-goers continued to attend performances of Franck's works. Unfortunately these were rarely of the oratorios, but the clamour for the Symphony and the *Variations Symphoniques* persisted all over England. In France and the United States also they became the twin pillars on which the composer's reputation rested. They maintain their popularity well into the 1970s. What is needed if Franck's reputation is to increase is a glut of performances and recordings of the lesser-known works—not necessarily the religious epics so much as such unexceptionable delights as *Les Éolides* and *Psyché*. There are distinct signs that something of this kind is happening. We may yet live to see this most ambiguous of composers associated with a quite different set of works from those with which he has been traditionally linked.

[1] Among his works is a 'Battle Symphony', tastelessly depicting the horrors of the Marne.

CHAPTER VI

SURVIVORS OF THE CIRCLE

MANY great composers were of special significance to their friends and acquaintances, seeming to reach the wider public through them and not so much through their own unaided efforts. Schubert may perhaps be counted among these. Possibly the same could be said of Elgar. Yet of neither of these might it be said that he perpetuated, through his musical friendships, a circle of important composers who not only shared the same aesthetic but helped to propagate it. Franck certainly stands out as the prime case in which an artist evolved a set of principles for the benefit of his co-artists, and where these principles seem to have led to the creation of a genuine *phalange*, or band of those dedicated to one another. It is possible to point to something of the kind after Franck's time, and in France too. Ravel's band of *apaches*—comprising himself, Ricardo Vinès, Henri de Régnier and one or two others—enjoyed a certain notoriety from their conjunction. But they were by no means all musicians, neither were they particularly successful in the absence of their founder. Henri Collet's *Les Six*—dubbed as such in 1920—were on the contrary all musicians, but really very artificial in their links. Honegger, Milhaud, Tailleferre, Auric, Poulenc and Durey were all briefly fashionable—and that was almost all they had in common. It is difficult even to this day to point to a group which had more personal involvement than the Franck group, and it is certainly hard to discover one that spoke so eloquently for itself on so many separate fronts. Before turning to the music, then, it might be desirable to comment on the various members who went to make up *la bande à Franck* and what it was that they owed to their founder.

With some deliberation I have entitled this chapter 'Survivors of the Circle', though there were a number of short-lived pupils of Franck who, despite their promise, failed to outdistance him, and will consequently be of greater interest to a biographer intent on resurrecting the circle's focus of interest. The majority, however, went beyond their teacher, some to such an extent as to bring their own names into public confusion with his. Vincent d'Indy, as we have had occasion to note, not only survived to write a highly controversial biography, but also headed a severe academy of music in which so much of Franck's teaching was passed on. We have it on the testimony of the same disciple that in all probability he would never have made a start as a composer had he not been assured of necessary prodding and (in his case) ruthless criticism from his master. For, whatever we may think of d'Indy today, only an ignoramus could discount the paramount role he occupied, whether for good or evil, in relation to nineteenth-century French music—and also during the first thirty years of the present century, when his influence may have been less but his presence was even more deeply felt. D'Indy was a focus of regional inquiry in music, a discoverer of Monteverdi, a born leader of all sorts of seemingly hopeless causes and, perhaps most of all, a quite advanced operatic composer whose definite notions of grouping and positioning on the stage put him a generation ahead of his contemporaries. These qualities are taken for granted in the 1970s, yet how many Frenchmen even appreciate what they owe to a man who came of age, musically, a hundred years ago? And will there not be someone enterprising enough to resurrect in full his huge corpus of music, so that we shall hear the operas (particularly *L'Étranger*) as well as the occasional tone-poem or *chanson*? Pianists, too, should be on the look-out for his charming *Tableaux de Voyage*, Op. 33, written to commemorate a journey in the Black Forest in his youth; the *Six Paraphrases sur des chansons enfantines de France*, Op. 95; and the unaccountably neglected *Fantaisie sur un vieil air de ronde française*, Op. 99. All of these and many more works help press for a d'Indy revival.

The average reader perhaps does not realize how much of d'Indy's personal fortune (he was a vicomte) he sank into various Franckist enterprises, nor the commendable manner in which he laboured to complete certain unfinished manuscripts of his fellow pupils. Charles Bordes's *Les Trois Vagues* was the most important of these, though unfortunately the least feasible proposition. But there were also symphonic poems by Chausson and Lekeu's *Quatuor inachevé*. D'Indy worked as hard on this last 'truncated masterpiece' as Lekeu himself had done (which is saying a great deal) and at least completed the second movement. Taking these things together, it could truthfully be said that few men would have given so freely of themselves at a time when they had their own careers to consider and when, as in the d'Indy-Lekeu case, there seemed a huge gap in age and attitude to overcome. It is a pity that d'Indy's later polemicism has given him the reputation of being a bigot, for he was what we should regard today as a musicologist of rare under-standing and a man dedicated to higher ideals than we force ourselves to make do with at present. He was a biographer of Beethoven and Wagner as well as of Franck, and the author of an enormous *Cours de Composition Musicale*—almost certainly the most influential treatise of its kind since Bazin's and not superseded until the publication of Messiaen's *Technique de mon langage musical* in 1944. He certainly did as much for French musical theory as did Sir Donald Tovey for English. Feuding with *Les Six* got him a bad name in the twenties, as did his persistent animosity towards Ravel. But it should be remembered that, despite a little show of superiority, he championed Debussy and shared with him much of that feeling for the French coast and countryside we all regard as familiar. Indeed Léon Vallas describes how Debussy—in his guise of Monsieur Croche—wrote a favourable notice of the première of *L'Étranger* which he saw at Brussels very shortly before embarking on *La Mer*.[1] This should be viewed as a significant portent.

Most authorities would say that, next to d'Indy, the musician whom Franck did most to promote was Henri Duparc, the song-writer and mystic. But Franck was a poor guide to the intricacies of the *mélodie*, its subtle metric clashes and recitative moving imperceptibly into *arioso*. Though a devoted Franckist and a tireless worker in the administrative cause of the Société Nationale, Duparc took most of his models in this sphere more from Gounod, Fauré and Lalo. Franck's much less-known pupil, Alexis de Castillon, may also have influenced him, though Castillon died at the age of thirty-four as a result of illness incurred in the Franco-Prussian War. Still, Duparc deserves mention if only for the sterling work he put in pleading Franck's cause while he was still regarded as an obscure organist. He must also receive his due for the extent to which he imbued other members of the circle with the authentic

---

[1] Léon Vallas, *The Theories of Claude Debussy* (Constable, 1969).

ideas of his teacher and himself. For instance he advised Chausson repeatedly over the writing of *Le Roi Arthus*, penning reams of criticism over the treatment of character and vocal creation. Some have questioned whether he did not go too far in this respect, claiming that much of his impotence rubbed off on his junior. It is difficult to say. But Chausson is certainly the next most important pupil to be considered, and one who did a great deal to assist the Franckist cause.

Seven years younger than Duparc, Chausson was a rich amateur who had no real need for music as a profession. Perhaps on account of his exalted station in life (his father had made a great fortune as one of Haussmann's building contractors) he none the less took his art tre-mendously seriously. What he learnt from Duparc was possibly the technique of the *mélodie*, for his *Serres Chaudes* (to poems by Maeterlinck), his Bouchor settings, and his odd choice of translated Shakespearean songs all helped to establish his reputation as one of the most accom-plished miniaturists in the group. He was, too, a would-be scaler of greater heights. Not only did he survive to complete *Le Roi Arthus*—which rather resembles *Tristan* in a more chaste and dutiful fashion—but he enriched the repertory with a major symphony that many good judges prefer to Franck's. This labour nearly cost Chausson his sanity, for he was not a natural musical giant. Still, he did what few Frenchmen have done in completing what is indubitably a fully scored and archi-tecturally sizeable work. Otherwise his *Poème* for violin and orchestra—predictably written for Ysaÿe—is well known even to those unacquainted with the Franckist movement, and is certainly his best-known composi-tion. It is successful largely because it is of exactly the right length, avoiding the *longueurs* of the symphony and the sometimes all too trivial congestion of the *mélodies*. Chausson was adept at chamber music as well, as the Piano Quartet testifies, and French music lost a rare spirit when his bicycle crashed into a wall at his country retreat, killing him instantly.

Among other older members of the Franck circle we should not fail to mention musicians like Samuel Rousseau (1853–1904), Augusta Holmès (1847–1903), Charles Bordes (1863–1909) and Gabriel Pierné (1877–1935). Amid the longer-lived were Guy Ropartz (1864–1955) and Pierre Onfroy de Bréville (1861–1949). All these wrote a good deal of music under the influence of Franck, but more importantly acted as disciples spreading his teaching and name to the provinces of France. Rousseau assisted in finishing Franck's posthumous opera *Ghisèle*, unstintingly helping Georges Franck to get it staged and reviewed. He also copied out the parts of many a Franck score while the composer was alive, earning his very special gratitude. Rousseau was a *Prix de Rome* winner, so that part of Franck's affection for him no doubt stemmed from the fact that he represented one of his more successful pupils. Mlle Holmès was a different matter. An Irish beauty, she is said to have captivated Franck to the extent of causing him to write the amorous music of the Piano Quintet and *Psyché*. We have no sure way of determining whether or not this is true, but Franck was certainly smitten by her looks and talent. Oddly enough, the music she herself wrote (including the *Ode Triomphale* and the opera, *La Montagne Noire*) is unremittingly masculine and nationalist in feeling. Bordes is notable for being one of the three founders of the Schola Cantorum a few years after Franck's death, and for being the great propagator of sixteenth-century contrapuntal music in France. He was among the finest choral conductors of the music of this epoch. Not only that, he was an authority on Basque music, and was given a commission by the government to investigate it. His activities as a composer were more modern, his works including settings of Verlaine and an impressive but unfinished opera called *Les Trois Vagues*. Even more versatile was Pierné, another *Prix de Rome* winner, who conducted for Colonne, deputized for Franck at the organ of Sainte-Clotilde and composed a wealth of vocal and instrumental music. Students today would do well to look at his neglected chamber works.

Of the above musicians none was as deeply involved with Franck as Ropartz and de Bréville, each of whom made it his business to teach the Franckist philosophy with particularly commendable thoroughness. Ropartz was quite self-effacing about this, going off to Nancy and Strasbourg where he headed the respective Conservatoires and preached Franck's gospel with unashamed fervour. His importance in disseminating the music of Franck can hardly be overestimated, since it was he whose contact with Ysaÿe made it possible to launch the Violin Sonata as well as many other works, including the String Quartet.

Ropartz's own music has a Breton flavour, and in this he imitated many another regional musician to have stemmed from Franck's little band. One of his earliest successes was a tone-poem entitled *La Chasse du Prince Arthur*, afterwards much admired by Honegger among others. But he wrote prolifically on a number of fronts, including in his output five symphonies, the Sainte Anne and Sainte Odile Masses, six string quartets, three violin sonatas, two cello sonatas and a long opera called *Le Pays*, which also depended for its appeal on a sense of regional nostalgia. Ropartz's *Concert Champêtre* is a good example of his semi-chamber style, beautifully expressive of the French outdoors. The relatively well-known *Prélude, Marine et Chanson* is another such piece, and one which it seems likely may have influenced both Ravel and Poulenc. As a teacher, Ropartz was decidedly less dogmatic than d'Indy, being willing to acknowledge any music that sounded well and was the product of serious labour. As his dates reveal, he lived to a remarkable age and was the last real survivor of the original school.

De Bréville lived almost as long, but undertook a different task. Attaching himself to the Schola staff as a teacher of counterpoint (in succession to Roussel) and chamber music, he helped shape the tastes of the new generation, or that part of it which had turned against the Conservatoire as being too concerned with producing mere executants. D'Indy never refrained from repeating that the Schola was to be a training ground in aesthetics, and he was consequently lucky that he was able to count on a man of de Bréville's high-mindedness to help him carry out his programme. A reserved figure, he had previously been suggested for the diplomatic service and was deeply patriotic in a quiet way. This is suggested by the fact that the First World War affected him powerfully and caused him to write a magnificent Violin Sonata in memory of Lt Gervais Cazes which gives the impression of being in the Franck-Fauré tradition. To many, however, de Bréville reached the pinnacle of his creative expression through his songs, of which he wrote almost as many as Fauré. Unfortunately a large proportion remain unpublished, and the composer cannot be said to have had his due from the public in this respect. Several of the songs are oriental in mood (like the striking *La Tête de Kenwarc'h*—a setting of Leconte de Lisle). Although Duparc warned him against becoming an exponent of the *mélodie* he does not seem to have taken the warning too seriously. Perhaps he was young enough to resist such an admonition in a way that Chausson would have found difficult. De Bréville and Chausson nevertheless have in common a certain charm not to be found among the majority of Franckists.

For the purposes of this study it is hardly worth listing Franck's many keyboard pupils, for most of them have failed to withstand the test of time. Arthur Coquard, who was a fellow student with Duparc at the Collège de Vaugirard, is of marginal importance and is remembered only through his gay opera *Le Troupe Jolicœur*. His contemporary, Albert Cahen, also turned to the theatre, but without any success. Most of his work was performed in opera-houses outside Paris, such as those at Rouen and Geneva. Camille Benoît, again, was a faithful follower, but his real career lay as a curator at the Louvre and the few belated works of merit which he wrote bear only a distant relation to Franck's. He was, in fact, a keen Wagnerian, and incurred Franck's wrath more than once by the apparently wrong-headed articles he wrote for his collection entitled *Souvenirs*. If gruelling tuition is the criterion, then Paul de Wailly deserves more mention since he had perhaps the most severe training Franck meted out. Unhappily he was not very progressive, as his pious oratorio *L'Apôtre* confirms. This appeared as late as the 1920s, when *Les Six* were in their glory. Almost certainly the best of Franck's lesser-known pupils was the Austro-Swiss composer Sylvio Lazzari, who had a brilliantly imaginative operatic mind, far too much ahead of his time. His *La Lépreuse* treated leprosy without fear or sentimentality, while the sensational *La Tour de Feu* became the first work staged at the Opéra to make use of a cinematic backcloth. It almost overshadowed *Götter-dämmerung*.

The musical public is at present displaying some interest in the careers of two of Franck's organ pupils who remained more or less domiciled within the Church—Louis Vierne and Charles Tournemire. Each of these held organ appointments throughout his life, Tournemire following in Franck's footsteps at Sainte-Clotilde and Vierne dying of a collapse after a recital at Notre Dame. They were both born in the same year— 1870—and consequently could not have derived from Franck anything but a superficial tuition. His example was probably more of an inspira-tion to them. Vierne certainly continued, in his organ symphonies, to build upon Franck's work as presented in the final *Chorals*, though with more harmonic and registrative originality. He was doubtless also in-fluenced by the fuller style of Widor, who succeeded Franck as professor at the Conservatoire, and stimulated these young men with his greater technical knowledge of the art of playing and composing for the instrument. Tournemire is perhaps of more vital concern to modernists today, for he was a powerful influence on Messiaen. Probably Messiaen derived his principle of the Trinity from Tournemire, and there is some internal evidence from among the works that he may also have acquired from him the technique of using transposed modes which he perfected. Indeed the combination of plainsong with post-Wagnerian harmonies is very characteristic of both composers, as is their avowed mysticism. Tournemire wrote a large quantity of music, including nine symphonies, none of which are played in France or elsewhere at the time of writing. In his *Combats de l'Idéal* he also had the interesting idea of taking three types of hero and painting their musical portraits. Don Quixote, Faust and St Francis of Assisi form the trio, and it is a pity that the composer's talents were not quite adequate for such dramatic ex-pression. Tournemire also wrote a complete set of *entrées* and *offertoires* for Sundays and festival days, and these have greatly enriched the organ repertory. Other organ pieces of his have been collected, including some which Maurice Duruflé jotted down from his improvisations at Sainte-Clotilde.

It is hard to be selective in naming pupils when a teacher had so many as Franck (some of them, like Debussy, were unwilling recruits to the organ class), but probably the most talented we have so far not con-sidered was the young Belgian, Guillaume Lekeu, chiefly known for yet another violin sonata. Lekeu was the last of Franck's really devoted pupils, even though their relationship was exceedingly short-lived and they died within a few years of each other. Lekeu was something of a polymath in that he was precocious in a way that no other Franck pupil had been. At school he had especially excelled in science and classics, while at university (he went to the Sorbonne) he chose to specialize in philosophy. With such a background, and with rich parents to guide him, it is remarkable that he turned to music. He owed it to Teodor de Wyzewa, the Mozart specialist, that he did not enrol at the Conservatoire but

NICOLAS-JOSEPH FRANCK

FRANCK'S HOUSE ON BOULEVARD ST MICHEL

Manuscrit de *Rédemption* (B.N. Section Musique).

MS PAGE FROM 'RÉDEMPTION'

COLLÈGE DE VAUGIRARD

THE OLD TROCADÉRO

THE CONSOLE AT SAINTE-CLOTILDE
bequeathed to Franck's pupil Charles Tournemire and now in the
possession of Flor Peeters

CÉSAR FRANCK IN 1890

MONUMENT TO CÉSAR FRANCK BY LENOIR AT SAINTE-CLOTILDE

instead took private lessons with Gaston Vallin, who had previously won the *Prix de Rome*. This was undoubtedly the right decision to have made, since Lekeu was much too advanced to benefit from the routine institutional type of course, while Vallin was known to Franck. The path was therefore soon cleared for a meeting, but it did not prove immediately fruitful. Franck by this time had tired of taking on more pupils and was half determined to reject this latest applicant. Whether or not the lad's Belgian nationality swayed the issue, or whether Franck simply could not face disappointing him, we shall never know. We do know, however, that he proposed an unusually high fee, and took it for granted that the lessons would form a short series. Actually, despite the great composer's death in 1890 and the fact that the two men did not get together until the autumn of 1889, it is clear that at least twenty or thirty lessons were given.[1] These were of a higher standard than any meted out to Franck's earlier pupils and were devoted largely to fugal writing, Lekeu having mastered all that was known about harmony, from the academic standpoint, from Vallin.

The relationship of Franck to Lekeu was really very much like that of father to son. Very little published work by the latter was written while he was under tuition, the only things he wrote being a plethora of fugal exercises and some chamber music involving the cello, two violins and cello, and full string quartet. None of these works was to make Lekeu's name and they are seldom heard today. Any complete survey of Lekeu's achievements is best placed in a biography of d'Indy, for it was he who assumed control of the young man's career once his idol was dead. The massive Piano Sonata, Violin Sonata and *Quatuor inachevé* do not therefore come within the purview of Franck's supervision, though they undoubtedly reflect his influence. Lekeu died of typhoid fever on the day after his twenty-fourth birthday without realizing the potential that all the members of the circle attributed to him. His presence in these pages is accordingly mainly to preserve the record, but also to indicate yet again what an extraordinary magnetism Franck possessed for even so great a prodigy as Lekeu, who, unlike the remaining figures of the band, was a

[1] This much is evident from examining Lekeu's letters to his mother and to Louis Kéfer, the director of the Verviers Conservatoire. See M. G. Lorrain, *Guillaume Lekeu, sa correspondance, sa vie et son œuvre* (Liège, 1923).

most unsaintly person, almost Beethovenian in his contempt for the un-talented majority and consistently scalding in his comments on all forms of academic music-making.[1] He was, perhaps, the earliest of the 'ex-pressionist' composers, and to Franck, the ardent composer of the Piano Quintet, must go some of the credit.

[1] I have not included in this necessarily superficial glance at the pupils those fellow travellers who attached themselves to Franck but were not in fact registered with him either at the Conservatoire or privately. Such figures include particularly Paul Dukas, Alfred Bruneau and Emmanuel Chabrier. They may also be said to include Saint-Saëns.

PART II

CHAPTER VII

THE PIANO WORKS

SINCE Franck began life as a prospective pianist it is only fitting that he should have contributed handsomely to the genre upon which his ambition was fixed. In his early days many virtuosi looked upon them-selves as composers. A line could be drawn from Chopin and Liszt to Anton Rubinstein to prove the point. Though considered primarily as a performer, therefore, Franck was given the warmest encouragement to compose for his instrument and even to play his compositions at the recitals he gave. These were hardly recitals as we know them today, but rather medleys of vocal and instrumental music amid which the odd piano fantasy generally found a grateful place. Only Liszt gave solo recitals, and even he was obliged to interlard them with transcriptions of popular airs of the day. In Franck's case the demand for transcriptions—or as often as not variations—of operatic material was constant and all-consuming. What pieces he played accordingly depended on what successes men like Hérold, Auber or Halévy might be having at the Opéra at that moment. These were the real musical heroes as far as the public were concerned, and they expected a concert to be a kind of warming-up process for the visit to the theatre they had been planning. The romantic age when pianists enthralled by virtue of their own talents was coming to a close in France, Chopin having retired ill to Nohant and Liszt having begun his stay in Weimar or his master-classes at the Villa d'Este. In the 1840s, therefore, the time was not propitious for the writing of pianistic masterpieces, and what we have to consider in Franck's early output is a series of *fantaisies* or *variations brillantes* in the style made popular by artists like Herz and Thalberg.

The second important fact to grasp concerns the actual chronology of his works. Because Nicolas-Joseph really expected his son would be an executant and not a composer he did not treat the sundry trifles he wrote with much seriousness. However, once it became apparent that the reverse was happening César's father revised the catalogue in such a way as to eliminate some of the works written before 1840, and to give greater prominence to the Trios which were composed at about that time. The result is hard to make plain. Originally the first two Trios were marked Op. 16 and Op. 22, but at this point Nicolas-Joseph decided to revert to Op. 1 once more. Hence an abortive catalogue exists, chiefly of piano music, which is extremely confusing since it has no real place in Franck's work, yet is sometimes referred to when dis-cussing his juvenilia.[1] Altogether eleven items are so indexed, though even these do not make up the full number of works written by Franck when a boy. They were not all published, but were bequeathed by Franck to Pierre de Bréville who in turn presented them to the Bibliothèque Nationale in Paris in 1947. There are some gaps in the numbers of this unrevised catalogue which we might suspect were left by Nicolas-Joseph so as to create an impression of greater size. Nothing of interest is contained in the first few numbers—an *Églogue, Grand Caprice* and *Souvenir d'Aix-la-Chapelle*. A transcription of four Schubert songs dates from about the same period. The *Églogue*, marked Op. 3, has a German subtitle, *Hirten-Gedicht*, or 'Shepherd's Song'. It was published by Schlesinger and dedicated to the Baroness Chabannes. In E minor, it gives little hint of the chromaticism we associate with Franck's late piano pieces, and is remarkable chiefly for containing wide stretches between the parts—a habit the composer may have formed because he had such large hands. However, the music looks occasionally as though it would have been better written for three staves, and in this Franck was certainly prophetic. True, Liszt had used this method, but in France it was still being regarded as revolutionary at the time Debussy wrote his second set of *Images* early in the present century. A *Ballade*, Op. 9, also appears at this point, and this is in Franck's more usual key of B major, though its *Allegro* section modulates to the tonic minor. The Schubert transcrip-tions incidentally include *The Trout* and *The Young Nun*, but are not

[1] The reader is advised that the very early works are not numbered, but the adolescent compositions here described were made to begin at Op. 3 so as to allow the late Trios to be first on the list.

treated with Lisztian pyrotechnics. All these pieces date from the period when Franck was having lessons from Reicha (1835–6) and therefore predate the Trios thereafter labelled Op. 1.

It scarcely seems necessary to say much about Franck's unpublished efforts. A *Grande Sonate* exists—indeed there were two. There was also a Rondo and a fantasy on themes from Hérold's opera *Le Pré-aux-clercs*. None of these found a place in the catalogue and were probably hidden away on Nicolas-Joseph's orders. On the other hand, a *Fantaisie*, which Franck wrote around the age of fifteen, evidently met with his approval, since it continued to be played. Franck even confessed to a sentimental liking for it in his maturity. This work should not be confused with the *Fantaisies* Op. 11 and Op. 12 on themes from Dalayrac's *Gulistan*. The latter are awarded a place in the catalogue, though they are hardly of any importance. What is striking about them is that they date from the time when Franck was striving hard to become a virtuoso and consequently they bear the marks of flashiness—dazzling arpeggios and the like—which he hoped would ensnare his audience. Franck was clearly learning from Liszt by this time, and there is another record (this time the work was not preserved) of his attempting to outplay Marmontel with a fantasy on Donizetti's *Lucia di Lammermoor*. Yet another *Fantaisie*, marked Op. 13, appears to have been lost or perhaps was never written. The only mature short piece for the piano Franck wrote before embarking on his first triptych was the relatively popular *Les Plaintes d'une Poupée* (1865). This *courte bluette*, as Jean Gallois has aptly called it, is not difficult, though like most French children's music it is not so easy as to be dismissed.[1] It is hardly as brilliant as the corresponding piece in Debussy's *Children's Corner*, of which it could be considered an anticipation, but these two composers tended to regard childhood with a similar wistfulness.

As has often been pointed out. Franck's piano production falls into two groups at either end of his career, and with the recently mentioned exception it is necessary to emphasize that once he had given up his pianistic ambitions around 1844 he appears to have forgotten about the instrument until 1884—a gap of forty years. Whether or not this is a fact

[1] It will be recalled that France has been especially rich in piano music for children, with contributions from Fauré and Ravel as well.

remains problematic. D'Indy stresses the fact that what sparked Franck off anew was his feeling, expressed to Conservatoire students, of deep dissatisfaction with the condition of the piano repertory—evidently not taking into account the masterpieces of Schumann, Liszt and Alkan. Perhaps this was the truth. On the other hand the Société Nationale had urged Franck to compose the Piano Quintet of 1879 (indeed one of his pupils, Alexis de Castillon, had written one some years previously), and it was only a step from there to penning a large work for the solo instrument. It was not, as some have supposed, a case of the *Prélude, Choral et Fugue* (1885) having grown out of the transcription for piano which Franck made of the *Prélude, Fugue et Variation* for organ. True, the composer had a knack of joining together forms normally existent on their own, but in this case what he planned was nothing so extended. It was allegedly merely a prelude and fugue in the style of Bach (not Mendelssohn again as others have imagined). When the composition grew, however, Franck became dissatisfied with the link between the Prelude and the Fugue and felt the need to intrude a slower section. That this section links up with the Fugue is a reflection of the composer's generally cyclical habits and Beethovenian tendency to economize on thematic material.

Despite the forty-year gap there can be no doubt that in this new work Franck found himself, as a composer for the piano, becoming one of that small company of men who have written really original and difficult works for the instrument. His position in this respect does not, of course, warrant comparison with Chopin or Debussy, but may be profitably regarded as resembling a less copious Brahms. Of the two triptychs he wrote the *Prélude, Choral et Fugue* is easily the more popular. Indeed it is indispensable to pianists specializing in the Romantic repertoire. Yet its successor was an equally demanding and rewarding work, and may still win the same wide appeal. Neither is an easy work to play. Their stretches make them inaccessible to the beginner, while the low octave basses suggest organ textures and are likewise difficult to hold beneath moving parts above. It is difficult to know what has endeared them to the public. They must certainly have been heartening to French pianists tired of the old round of operatic fantasies and transcriptions. On the other hand their best melodies shine with an effulgence Franck was capable of only on rare occasions—and this is as true of the manly *Choral* subject as of the tender *Aria* in the second of the two works. Saint-Saëns disapproved deeply of the former work, complaining that the *Choral* was not a choral and the *Fugue* not a fugue. This was partly a matter of envy and bad temper and partly a reflection of Franck's previously mentioned habit of allowing his material to coalesce in a rather individual fashion. Otherwise it has won acclaim from all the leading pianists of later generations, and has been a staple item in the repertoire of such a fine exponent of the period's music as Artur Rubinstein.

The theme of the *Prélude* of the 1885 work is a simple tune made complex by being embedded in a shimmer of arpeggios. The key is B minor, and above the opening tonic note in the bass lies a curious figure of seven demisemiquavers preceded by a rest. Yet the accent falls on the first of the group of seven, giving the movement a syncopated start. This accented note is also held down by an up-tailed crotchet, so that it has not just greater accentual force but longer duration than its companions in the bar. This pattern is then adhered to for the first four bars of the piece. It makes an imposing opening. In the second and fourth bars note-values are increased further where necessary. At the conclusion of this theme there is a change of mood: the music is marked *mf a capriccio*. This heralds a rather sad and slightly Brahmsian subject set high up in the piano's treble register in octave chords:

These chords move chromatically in a resigned vein until another *molto espressivo* theme—which is to be very important as a link in the work as a whole—takes their place.

As evidence of the cyclical form in which this composition is couched one has only to compare the second, Brahmsian, subject (Ex.1)—and its falling tones—with the link that leads from the *Choral* to the *Fugue.* The two themes may be juxtaposed in illustration:

The tonal descent henceforth becomes semitonal, intensifying by its chromaticism the whole tenor of the piece, which becomes something of a struggle between diatonicism and its opposite:

Meanwhile the first movement's exposition is conventional enough, with most of the development centring upon the arpeggio-like theme of the opening. The *Choral* contains an interesting pianistic device whereby the crossing of the hands enables the fullest octave chords to be given an extra unit in the treble. The theme itself is solemn and grave, rather like Chopin's famous *Prélude No. 20* and in the same key of C minor. Gallois [1] detects in it reminiscences of *Parsifal* and of Chausson's Piano Quartet. Its hesitant, meditative character is, however, more akin to one of the last three *Chorals* Franck wrote for organ, but sketched at an old piano.

Saint-Saëns was right to insist that the *Choral* breaks off into a more romantic texture: it eventually comes to rest on the single row of notes expressed in Ex. 2, designed to herald the fugue. From then on the tempo changes and triplets are substituted for the single crotchets of the intro-duction, the whole section being more animated and syncopated. The tonality of this last panel remains the most unstable, and the difficulties for the pianist, though very Lisztian, hint more strongly at Franck. The figuration of the *Prélude* and the *Choral* theme is heard again, but the most striking feature of the movement is its *bravura* cadenza, which Debussy parodied in *Dr Gradus ad Parnassum*. This ending has perhaps been the reason why virtuosi have chosen the work in preference to its fine companion.

Perhaps it is not too far fetched to observe a link between Debussy's trifling Valse, entitled *La Plus que lente*, and Franck's next work for piano —the small-scale *Danse Lente*. At any rate it is certain that Debussy's love of parody was to the fore when he wrote (at quite a late stage of his development) his little waltz, nowadays mainly the prerogative of amateurs. At the time of Franck's composition—that is to say in the late 1880s—Paris was glutted with slow waltzes of a sentimental cast, much as Edwardian England was to be. Debussy, with his individual sense of humour, called his parody 'the more than slow', probably because he wanted to indicate that if composers were to make their works much less spirited they would sink into a sludge of love-sickness. It will be recalled that it was he who had the nerve to provoke people to laughter at the love music of *Tristan* during part of *The Golliwog's Cake-Walk*. Doubtless

[1] *op. cit.*

there were other models than Franck's upon which Debussy sought to inflict his sarcasm, and it should not be thought that the younger composer was contemptuous of the older in any larger sense. On the contrary, Franck is one of the few who emerge with a fairly clean bill of health from *Monsieur Croche—Anti-Dilettante*, Debussy's pseudonymous attack on his predecessors and contemporaries. Moreover no one can fail to detect similarities between the two composers' string quartets. The *Danse Lente* survives mainly as a beginner's piece with nothing of the greatness of the two massive triptychs. It matches *Les Plaintes d'une Poupée*, rather than any of the earliest piano works, and is of no real importance in Franck's work. He was not adept at writing trifles, as was his enemy Saint-Saëns, and one cannot help being glad that his serious outlook was not directed to more works of this nature—of which there are already far too many in the repertory of French piano music.

When we reach the ultimate *Prélude, Aria et Final*, we are confronted with something infinitely greater—in fact a major sonata in all but name. It has not, as we have implied, achieved the same popularity as its companion, but this is not because it is noticeably more defective. It is possibly a shade more monotonous in its insistence on cyclical procedures, which are not used with the same variety of effect as in the earlier work. Otherwise there is little to choose between them. This second of Franck's pianistic masterpieces opens with, and continues to display, a primarily homophonic style. Though the part-writing is occasionally deceptive in its subtlety the final impression is always that of a harmonic and not a contrapuntal work. The opening movement has some striking key changes, showing how competent Franck was at both forms of writing. The theme, which constantly appears in old rondeau form, passes through E major, C sharp minor, E flat minor, E major and F major; the movement ends in the tonic key. It is one of the most memorable tunes Franck ever wrote, and it is surprising that this fact has not contributed to the work's greater popularity:

Ex.4

It has in common with the main theme of the first movement of the Violin Sonata a tendency to compensate for the direction in which its intervals flow, each phrase being followed by a slightly altered reflection. The thick basses which underlie this theme on most of its many appearances in the work suggest organ influences not apparent in the *Prélude, Choral et Fugue*. Contrariwise the *Aria* has some sweeping arpeggios that could only have been conceived for the piano. Its principal subject is a sixteen-bar phrase marked by an insistence on the descending fourth (a characteristic of the composition taken as a whole). In the *Final*, which also introduces the theme of the *Aria*, we discover some grand and very rhythmic pianism derived from Example 4. Its second subject is more bombastic and just pushes the work over into a piece of musical hyperbole. The quaver octaves in the right hand give it massive strength and the augmentation of the cyclical theme rounds the movement off with impressive architectural effect. While it is not quite the equal of the *Prélude, Choral et Fugue*, the *Prélude, Aria et Final* deserves to be played more often and is a good test-piece for an aspiring professional.

It is necessary to add a few words about Franck's piano style and its influence on the French tradition. Despite its confinement to two major works it is quite an individual thing. Utterly removed from the trifling *salon* pieces of Saint-Saëns, his compositions for the instrument seem equally distant from what we nowadays thinks of as typically Gallic keyboard music—that is to say music in which the soft, veiled tones are prominent and which conjures up comparisons with the painting of the Impressionists or *Intimistes*. We have already mentioned the name of Brahms, yet it is imperative to make clear that no mutual influences could have existed between these composers. The composer of the Variations and Fugue on a theme of Handel was generally abused in Paris and displayed customary rudeness by refusing to thumb through Franck's scores. Liszt, who once tried to act as an intermediary between them, was much more of a model for Franck. They knew one another intimately, and Franck's early efforts as a virtuoso must obviously have laid some of the foundation for his style. However, there is greater emphasis on musical ends in Franck's work, less display for its own sake. There is also a kind of baroque size and symmetry about it. Were it not for his greater *avant-garde* outlook, the composer most prefigured is Busoni. There is the same determination to see music as transcending the limitations of the instrument and aspiring to orchestral or even abstract sound. It is significant that in transcribing many of Bach's organ works for piano Busoni made use of a technique very similar to Franck's—characterized by wide stretches, deep-toned octave pedal-points and slightly congested part-writing. Both composers were great Bach-lovers who imported into their own scores some of the majestic vision of their idol. Busoni's works are now being resurrected by serious-minded musicians, recovered from the scrap-heap of pianistic panoplies left by the Rubin-steins and Godowskys and played as respectable contributions to the repertory. It is hoped that, in this enthusiasm for the monumental, Franck's magnificent essays will not be forgotten.

As the reader may have gathered, it was the style (or perhaps we should say styles) of Debussy and Ravel that triumphed in France in the early years of this century, leaving Franck's triptychs to stumble on like musical dinosaurs, or else be defended by the reactionary d'Indyistes. But it should be remembered that his work bore fruit which is perhaps receiving a little more favour now that the innovations of the Impressionists have been thoroughly absorbed. One thinks of the hour-long sonata by Paul Dukas who, though not a Franck pupil, most certainly imitated him in returning to large contrapuntal and architectural forms. His Rameau variations also make use of the typically Franckist procedure of binding together two or more classical ground-plans to produce a work of unique shape. Next to these might be de Bréville's single sonata—a more ingratiating work, but still full of Franckist devices. D'Indy's own E major Sonata is probably the most relentless of all such sequels to Franck's work—a piece more difficult to play than any of the compositions of other pupils on account of its consistently thick texture and awkward, unmelodious contours. Lekeu's Sonata for piano is again more like an ancient suite in its spread-out form, yet clearly purloined from Franck in its cyclical style. One can even trace Franckist influences on French piano music down to 1944, in Jacques de la Presle's neglected Theme and Variations—a work which mingles his procedures with those of Fauré, who also wrote in the variation form. This substantial legacy is still not greatly appreciated by a public which dotes upon the 'piece' as opposed to the 'work', the shadowy pictorial miniature as against the fugal or sonata structure. But it is much too substantial to be left out of account, and while musicologists re-examine the French pianistic inheritance it is inevitable that it will come more and more to light on the concert platform or in the recording studio.

CHAPTER VIII

THE ORGAN WORKS

To many people Franck is known chiefly as an organ composer, and though this reputation is unfair to him there is enough truth in it to make it plausible. Certainly he wrote many works for organ at all stages of his career, and not merely in the second part as was the case with so many of his other works. On the other hand it is arguable that Franck's organ composition sprang more from necessity than from inspiration. At least it falls within the period when he was actually an organist and a particular player of the instruments being produced by Cavaillé-Coll, the inventive genius who was to transform the organ by adding to it the modern manual coupling device and new flute and clarinet stops. Franck wrote his works at Sainte-Clotilde, which was widely regarded as Cavaillé-Coll's finest undertaking at the time it was built in 1858, and it can hardly be a coincidence that only two years after occupying this superb instrument Franck began the *Six Pièces* which comprise his first important works for organ.

The very titles of the pieces chosen are significant. Instead of the toccatas, fugues, preludes and so on, which made up the baroque repertory, Franck resorted to such names as *Pièce Heroïque*, *Pastorale* and *Prière*. Emmanuel Buenzod interprets this as a sign that Franck was already thinking in terms of the 'symphonic' organ, with its range of semi-orchestral effects and its overly secular repertory.[1] Actually he had been trained on the older Clicquot organs under Benoist at the Conservatoire, so that if this is so then he had practised assiduously on the new instruments from the moment they appeared. This is hinted at by the fact that he employed one of Pleyel's devices for training the feet to manage the heavier eight- and sixteen-foot stops. He had probably seen Hesse, the German organist, perform great feats and wished to emulate

[1] *César Franck* (Paris, Éditions Seghers, 1966).

74

him. His Belgian contemporary, Lemmens, was also among the quickest to attain celebrity on the new organs, and Franck is known to have heard him on several occasions. The upshot is that external factors had a special effect in inspiring Franck's first major pieces for the instrument. They were, in fact, his first really characteristic pieces of any kind, if we except the Trios of 1841. They remain among Franck's best works and are almost always to be found among the repertoires of all organists. The *Prélude, Fugue et Variation*, which was a new way of expressing the baroque type of piece, has indeed become famous not only in itself but in piano transcriptions by Franck himself and Harold Bauer.

The *Fantaisie* which begins the set is perhaps the most appealing to the ordinary listener. It is a meditative, quiet piece in the unexpected key of C major and sets the mood for the series in an admirable fashion. Buenzod comments: 'The Fantaisie in C and the five pieces which follow display a diversity, a liberty of accent, without equal in the amorphous style of the epoch.' [1] He also goes on to compare its contours with those of a typical Mendelssohn organ piece. There is certainly an affinity between these composers as may also be inferred from the fugal nature of their respective piano writing. Gallois, on the other hand, sees the *Fantaisie* as more in the tradition of the French overture. It is dedicated to Alexis Chauvet, then organist at La Trinité, and most of the remainder of the set also pay tribute to Franck's new organ friends, including Cavaillé-Coll. The *Fantaisie* is in three sections, with a central episode in *Allegretto* tempo flanked by two outer episodes. The initial *Lento* is rather too long to be part of a such a simple structure and contains little modulation. It has a canon slightly reminiscent of Brünnhilde's 'sleep' motif from *Die Walküre*, though it is impossible to imagine that there had been any influence. In the first section the effort went into creating a sober mood with which to begin the set; in the second some emphasis on colour is discernible. The theme engages in a dialogue of a rather attractive kind involving both the flute and trumpet stops. The latter stop was the best on the Sainte-Clotilde instrument, and it is probable that Franck wished to lose no time in displaying its excellence.

The next in the series is the *Prélude, Fugue et Variation*, a ternary

[1] *op. cit.*

structure in which the recapitulation takes the form of a variation. The prelude is formally a very loose section, free in its movement. The fugue is short and extremely simple. The variation is essentially melodic and does not attempt complex rhythmical or intervallic distortion. The *Grande Pièce Symphonique*, dedicated to Alkan, foreshadows the *Symphonic Variations* and the Symphony. In a sense it could be said that Franck, along with his pupil Vierne, inaugurated the 'organ symphony', and the title of this piece is highly significant. It could not have been so designated a few years earlier. It has been considered a trifle bombastic and it is not one to claim attention as being among the best of the series. It is in three movements, with an ample introduction of sixty bars, two antithetical themes and a strong rhythmic bias, unusual in Franck. The keys also represent a simpler outlook than we attribute to the mature Franck. The first theme is developed symphonically in the *Allegro non troppo et maestoso*. It is a somewhat inelegant tune, rough in its edges and not in keeping with the exquisite style of the *Fantaisie*. The second movement (*Andante*, with a middle section, *Allegro*) does, however, contain elements of serenity. A delicate balance between major and minor contributes greatly to the charm of this movement. To end, Franck unfortunately reverted to a form of *pompiérisme* or unashamed vulgarity. The movement is too loud and over-assertive and does not bring the piece to a very successful ending.

The *Pastorale*, dedicated to Cavaillé-Coll, contains much more delicate mixtures of tones and is basically centred upon two melodies, one a rhythmic sequence and the other a fine chorale. Oboe and flute stops are used with considerable freedom in this attractive movement, suggesting the naturalism of the countryside much as in Beethoven's *Pastoral* Symphony. There is a staccato central part (which sounds better on the piano), and this is again something of a sacrifice of good taste. The last part joins together the two initial melodies (a practice we find over and over again in all of Franck's works), and the illusion of bells suggests a possible Christmas scene imagined in a rural setting. This piece has a certain religious fervour despite its secular title, and is not in any way an expression of pantheism. The *Prière* in C sharp minor that follows was dedicated to Franck's master Benoist—a case of *bel hommage*. It is a very long prayer. Franck's improvisatory powers were evidently especially invoked as a tribute to his teacher, so as a result the work tends to be rather formless and a good deal of it is concerned with advanced modulation. The change to the major key (i.e. E major) is particularly radiant and typical of the composer:

Ex. 5   *Andantino sostenuto*

Last comes the *Final*, dedicated to the famous organist Lefébure-Wély. This is a bravura *morceau* as one would expect, since it is meant to round off the series. It is in what Buenzod calls the *mondain* style of organ writing.[1] All the sections conclude with a fanfare which recalls the ending of the *Grande Pièce Symphonique*. It is the case, therefore, that, despite the greatness of some of the pieces in this set, the set as a whole eludes success. It is

[1] *op. cit.*

worth playing and its best pieces are, as Léon Vallas has said, 'solidly mortised and mitred.'[1] But its weaknesses are also apparent and frequently weigh the set down.

There was to be a substantial gap between the 1860–2 *Six Pièces* and the next important works Franck wrote for the organ. These were the pieces commissioned for Alexandre Guilmant's recital at the newly opened Trocadéro. They were entitled *Trois Pièces* as anonymously as their predecessors, but they are a good deal less interesting. Composed in 1878, they show a gap of eighteen years following the works we have been discussing. During these years much greater emphasis was placed on the orchestral effects obtainable from the organ, which by now had lost all its baroque associations. Nevertheless Franck's first piece—a gentle *Cantabile* with a powerful climax—is strangely pianistic. The *Fantaisie* is not nearly as good as the one in the 1860 set and is much less often played —though one does occasionally hear it today. The themes are clear and the mood is properly established, but here again there is weak reliance on pianistic habits and the development section is extremely feeble. Comment on these two of the *Trois Pièces* suggests that Franck had not come to terms with the newly conceived ideas about the organ evolved by men like Saint-Saëns and Widor. It was their aim to simulate orchestral effects in a deliberate way, and they were proud of their achievements. Saint-Saëns even transcribed Liszt piano pieces for the organ, astounding the composer and establishing himself as one of the great masters of the new art.

Probably the best known of the three pieces for the Guilmant recital was the *Pièce Héroïque*, a genre in which Franck had never shown himself to be conspicuously successful. With its energy and insistence this piece none the less imposes itself on the memory, and there is hardly any question but that it is the best of three. The piece has two principal themes—one primarily rhythmic and the other melodic—and in this it imitates the inferior *Grande Pièce Symphonique* of the earlier period. It was to be twelve years before Franck would return to the organ, and then he had shed his flirtation with the 'symphonic' style.

The best of Franck's work is to be found again, and with more consistency, in the *Trois Chorals*, written in the last year of his life. These are

[1] Léon Vallas, *La Véritable Histoire de César Franck* (Paris, Flammarion, 1965).

introspective compositions, all redolent of the composer's tendency to mysticism. The first, in E major, though not the most popular, has perhaps the best opening melody of the series. The piece continues as a plain set of variations on this theme which, like earlier instances, tend to be straightforwardly melodic. The theme begins as follows:

Ex. 6 *Moderato*

The *choral* theme appears later, as a kind of pendant. This *choral* was written, like the others, on an old piano at Nemours on 7th August 1870, and it was only when Franck returned to Paris that he marked the regis- tration. It stands in the tradition of the seventeenth and eighteenth centuries in so far as it abandons all the slick devices of the new school as well as the patently transcribed style which had become intermediary in Franck's career. The variations were a subject of controversy with many strict musicians, who argued (much as Saint-Saëns had done in respect of the *Choral* in the *Prelude, Choral et Fugue*) that the work was consequently not a proper example of its genre. To their criticisms the composer answered somehow, even though he had neglected to ad- monish them in former years. His reply was: 'Vous verrez, *le vrai choral, ce n'est pas le choral; il se fait au courant du morceau.*'

Some of those who had taken him to task had actually been pupils, which may have been why his reply was so cautious. At any rate Franck (who rarely had a bad word to say for performances of his music and rarely a good word for the music itself) had a high opinion of this *Choral*, as well he might have. Though he was not destined to live long enough to know it, it and its companions had a profound effect on organ com- position in France, inspiring the tenebrous work of such men as Alain, Duruflé and their successors.

The first variation of the E major *Choral* is marked *cantabile* and is sharply characterized by its employment of the oboe stop. The quaver line is differentiated by the use of the flute stop. The whole variation is divided into short periods, the last of which re-states the theme of the *Choral*. By contrast the second variation (there are three altogether) is a majestic intermezzo. The harmony, very sombre in colouring, is a modulation taking the *Choral* as far away as G minor. It is not, however, as ambitious tonally as the third variation, which ranges over a variety of keys. Again, carillon effects are heard near the conclusion. The effect is ineffable and transfiguring. Altogether, despite there being three variations, each is divided into the periods we have mentioned. These are aimed chiefly at decorations and inversions, and the seventh period is generally regarded as the most elated. As an example of the kind of figuration Franck used in the first *Choral* we may quote the opening of the first variation, which shows the ease with which he derived a melodic extension of the main theme:

Ex. 7

By complete contrast the second *Choral*, which is in the key of B minor, is a grave and noble passacaglia. There is a short cadenza-like interlude in which Franck reveals his powers as a virtuoso of his chosen instrument. The tenor of the work is romantic despite this classical incursion, and the use of complex melodic suspensions tends to make it one of Franck's more closely textured works. The first two variations on the bass are in the tonic key; the third moves to the sub-dominant. Several of the subsequent variations preserve the shape of the theme without actually presenting it. One of them, in B major, offers us a glimpse of the Franck of the Christ motif of *Les Béatitudes*:

Ex. 8

The quiet interplay of parts of this second *Choral* also makes it reminiscent of the *Prière* of 1860-2, especially in the hesitant interruptions in which it abounds. It seems, like the earlier composition, to be striving for some answer—not in fugal terms but in terms of the ultimate. In the view of some critics the second *Choral* should be construed as a *cri humain*—a kind of supplicatory work in its questing after a response to man's predicament. If one takes this view its close inspires one to think of it as a victorious work, having overcome passion (the intermezzo) and reached repose.

Common consent accords the laurel to the *Choral No. 3* in another key not much used by Franck—namely A minor. Its principal theme is very simple:

Compared with its predecessors, it seems on the face of it a model for one of the composer's offertories. This critique—if that is what it is—could be levelled to a lesser degree at No. 1. Be that as it may, No. 3 has achieved the greater popularity. It is a staple item in the repertory of every competent organist. Written in tripartite form, it seems to some to be a classical sonata, an *adagio* couched between two *allegros*. Rather, however, the third section offers itself as a *grand da capo* in which the two previous themes are resumed. The quasi-allegro introduction to the work takes the form of rapid figuration and is virtually unaccompanied:

There is a melodic element to these arpeggios, and it should not be thought that the chorale theme is the only one in the entire work. The *allegro* is followed by a beautiful *adagio*, very song-like in character. It is marked *dolce espressivo* with a solo for oboe and trumpet. The accents continue to be syncopated, and there are brief echoes of the chorale. This section is both fragmentary and unified, one of the most subtle, if simple, that Franck ever wrote. The conclusion is bold, with the large affirmative chords we have come to expect from Franck's finales. It is tonally adventurous, and ends on a *Tierce de Picardie* in A major.

Most of Franck's other works for organ were combined with instruments or voices and do not really merit special comment. They were written for ecclesiastical or occasional purposes, displaying little of the composer's unique feeling for the organ. He did, however, leave posthumously a collection of fifty-nine versicles collected under the general title *L'Organiste*. These add noticeably to his canon while being too great in number to merit individual analysis. They show that, whatever his aims were in the *Chorals* (and he is reported as saying 'I am going to write some *Chorals*, like Bach's, only with a different plan'), his last thoughts were directed towards the simple church ends which he so much revered. In fact the *Chorals* stand rather in the tradition of the late Beethoven quartets and sonatas. The versicles, on the other hand, are pure Franck and have likewise left an important legacy to French composers such as Messiaen and Tournemire, both of whom wrote complete sets of offertories for Saints' Days and Weekdays. Franck was never a supreme performer on this instrument (Maurice Emmanuel insisted he was better as a pianist), and it was his love of the church and the organ loft that really inspired him.[1] His virtuoso pieces, the *Chorals* apart, are mixed and on the whole less successful than his reputation would have us believe. What is great and timeless about Franck's organ works is the simplicity of their design, the atmosphere of religious and poetic faith they proclaim.

[1] *César Franck* (Paris, Laurens, 1930).

CHAPTER IX

THE CHAMBER MUSIC

FRANCK never achieved anything in any genre comparable with the set of Piano Trios written around 1841. Students of chamber music in France will be hard put to it to discover other examples of this type of music, so common in Germany, belonging to the period. Franck cannot be regarded as the originator of such music in his country. Couperin and his followers had written for intimate combinations a century earlier. But there can be no doubt that if we equate chamber music not with the baroque sonata or rococo serenade, but with the taut Beethovenian form, then Franck was indeed its pioneer. Alongside him we should, of course, mention the lesser-known names of Lalo, Alexis de Castillon and even Saint-Saëns, but none of these successfully created a medium to rival the works of, say, Schumann or Brahms; whereas Franck eventually did. As in the pianistic sphere, however, what we perceive in looking at his complete output is a cluster of works at each end of his career, the earlier being inferior to, if predictive of, the later. The difference is that, while the piano works can easily be related to his training and platform presence, the first chamber works came out of the blue. We can only assume that assiduous study of the scores of Beethoven and Schubert taught him, as they did Brahms, the knack of writing as forcefully and brilliantly for the smaller ensemble as for the larger.

The first of the Trios (which were originally three, but which later grew into four) was designated Op. 1, No. 1 and was set in the key of F sharp minor—already something of a portent for those who were prepared for lengthy excursions in the tonic major, one of Franck's favourite keys. The significant feature of this first Trio is the confident use of the cyclical method which it displays. The opening figure on the piano, consisting of four crotchets (F sharp, G sharp repeated and F sharp), becomes a cell that recurs in many rhythms and contexts. The cello theme which enters above this, with its sustained semibreves, also reinforces the method. But it is the bass counter-subject that is really significant. It suggests a slightly inquie insistence probing its way throughout the entire composition. The models for cyclical techniques are not impossible to find, though they do not occur in France. Beethoven's Fifth Symphony, with its soft recurrence of the *Scherzo* motif in the finale, is a case in point. There are also many instances in his late quartets, as in Schubert's E flat Quartet. Still it was a daring procedure for a composer of eighteen to adopt. It also tends to establish Franck's precedence over, say, Liszt as an innovator in this sphere. Both composers used the technique to great advantage, but in the case of the Romantics it was Franck who led the way.

The habit of straying into the tonic major is also evident in the Trio, as we have implied. The following example from a later section of the first movement is an illustration of this:

Ex. 11   *Andante con moto*

This example is interesting, too, because it reveals so clearly the composer's typical preference for step-wise melody, rising and falling in a manner that would scarcely seem melodious and yet succeeds in being altogether memorable. In this he was imitated by both Fauré and d'Indy, the latter often choosing apparently banal folk-song material in which the intervals posed no sudden angularity. Note that the accompaniment to this figure suggests once more the influence of Beethoven and Schubert—clearly the main claims on Franck's attention at this time.

The Scherzo of the first Trio is remarkable for having two trios, a case very rare in chamber-music literature. D'Indy, in his essay in *Cobbett's*

Franck

Cyclopedic Survey of Chamber Music, points out that the same ploy was used by Schumann in his B flat Symphony, actually written in the same year. Whether this was coincidence or not no one can tell. The final recapitulation of the Scherzo, which includes a reference to the cello theme of the first movement, is varied and leads into the finale. A further indication of the cyclical style is that the F sharp major theme from the first movement (Ex. 11) provides the material for the second trio. Of the finale, we can say that it is the most ambitious of the three movements, architecturally traditional and again presenting the two main themes of the first movement. Keys as remote as D flat minor and D major are reached in this movement, and the entire work ends triumphantly. Aside from those already mentioned, the main influences seem to have been Weber, Lesueur and Cherubini. The mood of the work is sombre: the critic, Maurice Bourges, once compared it rather strangely to the English taate for the macabre. Perhaps this—and occasional clumsinesses in the writing—is what has consigned the work to oblivion. Still, with the exception of the one-movement fourth Trio it is the most important in the set.

The second Trio was called the 'Trio de Salon' by Franck himself, and this gives a good indication of its much less pioneering manner. It is meant to please the less discriminating public and contains some gracious if saccharine tunes. One unusual feature is the sturdiness of the chordal writing for the piano. Here, for the first time, we get a glimpse of the massive hands for which Franck was famous and which he probably inherited from his father. It does not nevertheless suggest very strongly the aggravated compositions of later decades such as the Piano Quintet—a work even more full of huge stretches and thunderous octave passages. The third Trio was originally the final member of the set and was marked by its more contrapuntal character. It is certainly much less congested than its predecessor. It is again cyclical, but this time also rather unbalanced, its last movement being outstandingly fine and long. It was this that caused Liszt to advocate abstracting it and making it a fourth Trio on its own—a course the composer followed without demur. This fourth work is very chromatic, and in the recapitulation the second subject is presented before the first—another unconventional touch. Academic critics will find a pair of consecutive fifths hidden away in it.

The Chamber Music

The next great stride forward in chamber music was inexplicably delayed by forty years—or, to be more exact, to 1879, when the Piano Quintet made its first promptings. This is one of the most remarkable compositions in the entire literature of chamber music, so crammed is it with stark emotion and complex cyclical form. On the latter count it has even been suggested that one of the themes from the F sharp minor Trio was imported, carrying the cyclical principle to its utmost limits. A deeply felt work, it begins appropriately with an introduction for strings alone. This section of the work is marked *molto moderato quasi lento*, thus making it a slow beginning:

Ex. 12

To this a plaintive response is made, as in the *Variations Symphoniques*. This whole section can be viewed as an introduction to a sonata form movement, if so desired. For the second group includes a pivotal theme, which centres upon a B natural in the key of F minor and gives the work a peculiar tonal twist. It is followed by a low-pitched theme, beginning on a semiquaver F in the bar before, and this, too, has some significance as a recurrent element in the composition. These two may be considered complementary cells. Finally, with another theme, descending from A flat to F, and then again from D flat to A flat (there is a persistent drooping quality about this first movement), the exposition of themes ends. A dialogue follows and the themes are repeated in a variety of keys; the unexpected note in the second group now comes dangerously on to F flat. The next movement is an *Andante douloureux* in ternary form, and is one of Franck's more extended interludes (see for comparison parts of *Les Djinns* and the *Variations Symphoniques*). The finale is once again powerful and erotic at the same time. The cyclical interest now stems from the fact that the extended coda takes its main theme from the coda of the first movement and also the development section of the slow movement. All in all the work is a triumphant *chef d'œuvre*.

Of the remaining chamber works, it would take a connoisseur to say which was the finer. Gallois calls the Violin Sonata a Cartesian work, presumably thinking of its incredibly beautiful balance between the two instruments.[1] It is certainly among the supreme treasures of Franck's works. In four movements in sharp contrast to the usual three it can be compared with the Brahms D minor. Originally Franck wanted the initial movement played slowly, but on hearing Ysaÿe play it faster gave his blessing to the marking *Allegretto*. After some gentle chords on the piano the violin enters with a typical undulating theme in which an arpeggio is played both forwards and backwards. The interval of a third gave Franck the basis for this most mellifluous movement. Many commentators have likened this opening to the famous passage in Proust's *Swann's Way*, where the author likens the instruments to the call of a bird to its mate at the heralding of the dawn. Proust certainly admired Franck's work, and both this and the String Quartet may have served as models for works by the fictional composer Vinteuil. Unusually for Franck, the first movement of the Sonata remains serene and unruffled. It is a kind of homage to nature, and not as forceful as the passionate first movement of Fauré's first sonata which preceded it by a decade. It is with the *Allegro passionato* that force is first employed. Here it is the piano which dictates the pace. In this it resembles the figuration of a Chopin or Liszt *étude*. The whole movement is *une brutale explosion* which contrasts excellently with the smoothness of the first.

Now appears a Bach-like *recitativo* movement which some have considered out of place in a work so Romantic. It is marked *Quasi una fantasia*. Why did Franck include it one wonders? Possibly because of his desire to redirect chamber music back to the older forms, and possibly out of an infatuation with Bach's organ works which he could not

[1] *op. cit.*

refrain from suppressing. Parts of the recitative are unaccompanied violin cantilena, however, so that if there was a model it must have been that composer's unaccompanied partitas. Whereas the second movement's fierce piano *ostinato* was accompanied by soaring emotional melody on the violin this third movement is severe and classical. Formally, too, it contrasts, the earlier being in simple ternary form as opposed to the free fantasia of the later. The fantasia gives the impression of an improvisation, and to some critics is out of place in so obviously effulgent a work as the Violin Sonata. Yet it provides contrast and brings greater dignity to the form that other composers had created with such light-heartedness. Certainly it is a far cry from the minuet or over-sentimental *andante* often placed in this position in a sonata. In the *fantasia* three episodes are generated and developed. They are all mysterious and slighty elegiac. The whole seems a peculiar enigma which is dissipated only when we reach the fourth page and a greater clarity of vision begins to emerge. Like most of Franck's improvisations this movement also passes through a succession of keys.

The last movement begins with a canon that is possibly the best-known example of the device ever to have been written outside the works of Bach. Franck was brilliant at canonic writing, as some of the *Six Pièces* had already shown, and this example seems even more natural and unforced than any in the organ set. It brings a feeling of immense stability to the conclusion, uniting piano and violin again but in such a way that one feels they have never been separated. Some critics have noted a resemblance between this theme and that of the *chœur des anges* from the cantata *Rédemption*. It is possible that they are correct, though Franck's small slivers of thematic material, however memorable they may be, often have many elements in common. This is no doubt why he has so often been accused of plagiarizing material from Beethoven or Schubert or one of his other exemplars. The form of the canonic finale is that of an old French rondeau, a device much used and admired by members of the circle. This form, together with the simple beauty of the writing, combines to lend an atmosphere of harmonious perfection to the work admirably suited to bringing about its conclusion. Here overleaf is the canonic theme in illustration of Franck's almost unique power of simplicity:

Ex. 13 *Allegretto poco mosso*

dolce cantabile

dolce cantabile

Quite possibly the Violin Sonata is Franck's greatest work. Robert Jardillier, in his analysis of the composer's chamber music, offers the interesting suggestion that the opening theme of the first movement had its origin in Gregorian chant. He also regards it as the motto theme of the work, though the sonata is by no means as cyclical a composition as the Piano Quintet. However, the first movement does not really have a development section, so that some other explanation than the usual sonata-form description must be given. The play from C sharp to C natural in its main theme is perhaps the mainstay of the movement, just as the pivotal play with the B flat and B natural made up one important strand in the quintet. *Ostinato* is also a habit of the *Allegro*, but in a larger sense, the whirling piano figuration constantly providing the groundwork for the violin's flights. The *fantasia* must consequently be seen as largely a harmonic and contrapuntal exercise—the main modulation is from D to the favoured F sharp. What is so striking about the finale is the astonishing balance between the instruments—each of which is complemented at every turn. Its single failure lies perhaps in the coda, where for the first time in this sublime work Franck gives in to sheer virtuosity. The climbing octaves in the bass part of the piano become reminiscent of one of Liszt's operatic transcriptions, and the whole harks back rather obviously to the ideals of Franck's days as a virtuoso. The same criticism was made, as will be recalled, of the *Prélude, Choral et Fugue*, in which a slightly cheap ending spoilt an otherwise superb composition. As the coda is shorter and more natural in the sonata it seems less damaging.

Franck's last and crowning achievement in the sphere we are considering was his String Quartet, the only work for which he had something close to sincere acclaim. It took him many months to write, especially the long first movement which d'Indy has described as a 'sonata form within a *lied*'. The movement begins in D major with what d'Indy calls a *thème générateur*, having the characteristic falling thirds:

This slow introduction is followed by the exposition of a sonata *Allegro* in D minor. There are three themes, two in D minor and the third in F major. At the point where the development would normally occur the *thème générateur* is introduced in the form of a *fugato* in F minor. A modulation and a quickening of the pace lead to a resumption of the *Allegro*, the development of whose material begins in G minor and passes through a variety of keys. The recapitulation of the sonata movement follows, at first in D minor and eventually in D major. A coda is provided by a shortened version of the slow introduction.

By contrast the second movement is conventional in structure. It is very youthful in spirit and took Franck a mere ten days to write. Emmanuel Buenzod considers it original, not following the practice of any previous composer, as for example the first movement tended to follow the unorthodoxies of the late Beethoven quartets. He suggests that possibly Berlioz's *Queen Mab* might have had an influence on it, but is otherwise adamant. The interest of this movement is essentially rhythmic, the zigzagging of the parts being rather unusual in the composer's works. Far more brusque and lively, it acts as a suitable foil for the two serious movements it separates. The trio—which this time is a single entity—has the shape of a barcarolle. Vincent d'Indy described this enchanting movement as a 'ronde de sylphes dans un paysage sans lune.'

The third movement is the most sovereign of all, being a solemn *Larghetto*. It was Franck's *pièce de résistance* in the chamber-music field, and he worked hard at it, exclaiming enthusiastically to d'Indy that at last he had got it right and that it was very beautiful. The refrain (a 32-bar phrase) is slightly reminiscent of the Violin Sonata and the *Prélude, Aria et Final*. This is worth noting because of the resemblance of the second movement to parts of *Les Éolides* and *Psyché*. The *Larghetto* is severe, passionate music (it again appealed greatly to Proust, who had the Poulin Quartet play the work for him privately in his bedroom) and all the instruments are used more or less throughout. It is, in this sense, absolute music. Norman Demuth said of it: 'This movement is as great as any of the slow movements of the later Beethoven, Schubert and Brahms.'[1] It certainly has their seriousness, and is possibly the best single movement Franck ever wrote, along with the canonic finale of the Violin Sonata.

The last movement of this magnificent work is perhaps the least interesting. In it Franck rounds up the various themes from the other movements in a large and almost bombastic *mélange*. It is a forceful movement, but it lacks the individuality of the others, some of which cost the composer so much effort. Franck indeed always found it easier to

[1] *César Franck* (Harrap, 1949).

recapitulate material than to invent it. However, the Quartet viewed as a whole was extremely influential and important. Debussy's single Quartet—which it incidentally closely resembles—appeared within a few years while Ravel's (which also used the cyclical technique) appeared only just over a decade later. These were merely the best known of its fruits. We must also think of the quartets of Magnard, Roussel and d'Indy —all of whom took Franck as their model—and the massive *Quatuor inachevé* of Lekeu, which would surely have been a significant addition to the tradition had it been completed. Franck therefore not only initiated chamber music as we know it in France, but he also bequeathed the most important legacy in that sector with the possible exception of Fauré, whose works (especially the Piano Quartets and Quintet) were greatly underestimated. Of all the genres in which he wrote it is tempting to regard chamber music as Franck's greatest achievement, his supreme legacy to the world of French music that was to spring up during the years of the First World War and after.

CHAPTER X

THE ORCHESTRAL WORKS

On no account can Franck be considered a prolific composer after the fashion of Massenet or Saint-Saëns. The extent of his work for his chosen instruments—the piano and the organ—is hardly sizeable. Ironically he composed more for the orchestra and for voices, and his work for the former medium is easily that which has brought him the greatest fame. As had happened with some of the other media, Franck began his orchestral catalogue early, only to postpone the remainder until the age of fifty-four. He has frequently been charged with writing for the orchestra as if it were an organ (pausing as if changing from Swell to Great and so on), and though there is a grain of truth in this it would be absurd to claim that he was not a master of orchestral technique. It is probable that he would have written much more freely for the medium had he not pinned his hopes for too long on church music. During the period when the circle was at its most reverent it was considered a trifle jejune to write for orchestra alone, and there were some disciples who actively discouraged their master from taking this line. This was especially true when one reflects that many of his orchestral tone-poems were based on pagan myths or picturesque subjects. Contempt for such themes was a feature of the attitudes of many of Franck's friends, even though they paradoxically used such themes themselves from time to time. However, the composer had learnt to be independent of public opinion and he quietly went his own way in building up an impressive corpus of orchestral pieces, most of which remain in the repertory to this day.

In about 1845–6 Franck began the first of his symphonic poems. It was based on Hugo's verses and was entitled *Ce qu'on entend sur la montagne*. It is tempting to follow Julien Tiersot and claim that in this work Franck invented the genre. Unhappily that honour almost certainly goes to Liszt who, though his work on the same subject was not completed till 1849, had made sketches for it in the 1830s. Liszt also achieved publication and performance first. Indeed it was the failure of Franck to find either a publisher or a means of performance that killed the work. Still, he deserves some credit for having independently reached a medium of such importance, especially to French music. Liszt's *Ce qu'on entend sur la montagne* became the first of a dozen symphonic poems, so that his claim is also enhanced by sheer bulk. Franck, on the other hand, did not return to the genre for thirty years. It is impossible to say whether this was out of disappointment or preoccupation with other things. We do know that he suffered a mild nervous breakdown about the time of its composition, but this is attributed by d'Indy to the especially arduous teaching commitments he was saddled with.

The subject of Hugo's poem is the contrast between two cosmic voices—one springing from the sea and the other from the land. The sea voice is full of life and joy, while the mother-earth voice is full of the sadness of those who suffer on the soil. The object seems to be a revelation of the gulf that exists between Nature and Human Nature—the former constantly triumphing over the latter. It is a typically Romantic notion which found expression in a great deal of the poetry of the time. Hugo describes the two voices thus:

> L'une venait des mers; chant de gloire! hymne heureux!
> C'était la voix des flots qui se parlaient entre eux;
> L'autre, qui s'élevait de la terre où nous sommes,
> Était triste: c'était le murmure des hommes.

> (One came from the sea: a song of glory, a hymn of happiness.
> It was the voice of the waves talking to each other.
> The other, which rose from this earth of ours,
> Was sad: it was the murmuring of men.)

Franck's music, beginning in E major, is slow and gentle with prominence given to the woodwind. It is almost an impressionistic work and to that extent anticipates *Les Éolides*. One unusual effect is the conscious attempt to use the orchestra to create a contrast between 'le chant de la nature' and 'le cri humain'. Notable, too, is the insistent use of the augmented fourth. The second theme shows a resemblance to Liszt's *Les Préludes*, written a few years later.

The scoring of *Les Éolides*—for orchestra without trombones—is more modest. It accordingly avoids the *fortissimo* climax which is a characteristic of *Ce qu'on entend sur la montagne*. Aside from Mendelssohn's music for *A Midsummer Night's Dream* its nearest relative is surprisingly Debussy's yet unwritten *Nuages*. Though the work was partly inspired by the mistral (experienced while the composer was on holiday at Valence), the classical basis requires explanation. The Aeolids were apparently a race of fleeting fairies who inhabited the mountainous regions and swooped down occasionally on to the lowlands. The poem by Leconte de Lisle upon which Franck based his *scherzo* mentions

> Brises flottantes des cieux ... qui de baisers capricieux
> caressant les monts et les plaines. ...
>
> (Floating breezes of the skies ... implanting kisses with
> fickle tenderness on the mountains and the plains.)

The episodes in the work are loosely tied, but Franck imbued them with his customary canonical devices. It is at once the most charming and the most strict of compositions. The woodwind is particularly adroitly used, as the doubling of the clarinets at one point shows. In also doubling the melody at the fifteenth, Franck appears to be anticipating Ravel. The 'breeze' theme comes after a languid introduction and may strike the listener as quite unlike the composer. Elsewhere he has been justly accused of polarizing his themes around a single note. Here, as we can see, the intervals are wide and any amount of air is let into the music:

Ex. 15

The remainder of the work is firmer though still retaining the gossamer-like qualities which were later to be reproduced in *Psyché*. To conclude,

Franck resorts to a more familiar habit—that of mixing the themes together in a fairly heavy stratum of counterpoint. Taken in all, however, *Les Éolides* must rank among his few masterpieces.

Le Chasseur Maudit, which was the next of Franck's orchestral works, could not have been more different. The most ribald of his compositions, it was probably meant to be taken seriously but has lapsed into a comic vein with time. About a count who forgoes St Hubert's Mass to go hunting, it depicts the chase in blatantly imitative music and ends with the unfortunate huntsman being pursued into Hell by a horde of devils. Obviously the work has a moral, but it is one that no longer holds much sway in a time when church-going is the exception rather than the rule. Based on a ballad by Bürger, it embarrassed the master's pupils and perhaps dissuaded him from attempting anything quite so picturesque again. A long but well-balanced work, it opens with the following hunting call:

Ex. 16 *Andantino quasi allegretto*

The summons is taken up: instead of attending the church (whose choir can be heard in the distance) the count thunders past it in search of his prey. This part of the music becomes so loud and obstreperous that it threatens to drown all the other references Franck intended. Though there is too great a reliance on the cellos, Franck gives us some good flute and bassoon writing, and there are two *cornets à piston* in the score to add brilliance. The main subject of the *galop* is as irresistible as that of Dukas's *Sorcerer's Apprentice*:

As in the latter work the ending is a *tutti* from the full orchestra. It is difficult to know where Franck found the model for *Le Chasseur Maudit*. The author of the poem is the same as Duparc had used for *Lénore*. Yet one senses a harking back to one of the composer's earliest exemplars—namely Meyerbeer. In any case it is easily his most tumultuous work.

In considering *Les Djinns* we must admit an intruder into the orchestral ranks in the shape of a piano *obbligato*. That it does not assume solo pro-portions is only another indication of Franck's restraint and his un-conscious capacity for innovation. It will be recalled that a similar layout was conceived for works like d'Indy's *Symphonie Cévenole*, Fauré's *Ballade* and *Fantaisie*, and Richard Strauss's *Burleske*. Unlike the two previous symphonic poems Franck had recently written *Les Djinns* is not immediately meaningful: its theme is insufficiently graphic to impose itself without reference. It was based upon a poem from Hugo's *Les Orientales*, but given a quasi-Christian interpretation. The poem is an attempt at *diablerie* and depicts dead souls shrieking from their resting-place. The subject is akin to that of Saint-Saëns's *Danse Macabre*. It is so

The Orchestral Works

untypical of Franck that when Colonne came to conduct it he called out to the composer: 'Ça vous plaît, ça?' Franck's reply was simply: 'C'est affreux, continuons.' However much Franck may have been influenced by Saint-Saëns in his choice of subject, the idea of using the piano *obbligato* was one that was put to him by Mme de Serres, or Mlle Caroline Montigny-Remaury as she was better known. She was Ambroise Thomas's sister-in-law and her word carried the weight of a command. When she asked for a short *concertante* work she unwittingly gave Franck the idea for this new style of composition.

The work itself is in something close to sonata form, with two major themes—one symbolizing the devilry and the other the forces of good. Their opposition gives the work its sense of movement and conflict. The orchestra begins with a wild, sinister scherzo-like tune, partly martial in character, which introduces the main idea. Later the piano enters with a swirling accompaniment and makes repeated entries in the development. It is interesting to note that Franck reversed Liszt's notion in the *Malédiction* by choosing the piano to prefigure the good and the orchestra the bad. The calming effect of the expressive piano interludes leads to a recapitulation and a brief virtuoso coda. The work is difficult for pianists on account of the wide stretches and double octaves involved.

As if in grateful reparation for his playing of *Les Djinns* Franck wrote a second piece for piano and orchestra—this time giving the piano far more prominence—for Louis Diémer, the assistant to Marmontel. This new work was the *Variations Symphoniques*. The first thing to note about it is the reappearance of Franck's habit of harnessing together two essentially different classical forms. In this case he even went one better by providing the work with two themes for varying. The exposition of the first theme—a tremendously dramatic and tense unison structure—is left to the strings. A drooping reprise comes from the piano at the ends of its phrases. The whole makes much use of sequence, a device to be found in profusion among Franck's works. The second theme is heard first on *pizzicato* strings and woodwind. This is a beautiful *cantabile* melody in 3/4 time with a plethora of rests which are later filled out by figuration. The theme is shown overleaf:

Ex.18

Flutes & Violins

Poco allegro

After further discussion of the first theme the piano presents a slightly different and more extended version of the second. Five variations of the second theme follow without any break between them. The first is a dialogue for strings and piano with discreet touches from the woodwind. The second variation assigns the theme to violas and cellos with a double-bass pedal. The third variation is one of the most decorative for the piano. By the fourth variation some of the material of the dramatic introduction is inserted, allowing for a certain rhythmic freedom. It continues into Variation V. As in *Les Djinns*, Variation VI comes as an emotive interlude which first presents the theme in the major. The finale is a brilliant peroration based on the first theme, with incidental references to the second.

The last of Franck's symphonic poems—it does go by this description and not that of cantata—is his setting of the myth of *Psyché* for choir and orchestra. It is in two parts, the first comprising *Sommeil de Psyché* and *Psyché enlevée par les Zephyrs* and the second *Les Jardins d'Éros*, *Le Châtiment* and *Apothéose*. The opening theme, revealing Psyche asleep, is slow with a pulsating chordal accompaniment.

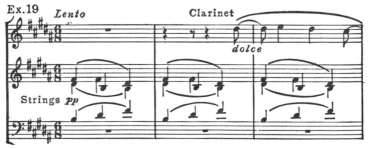

Ex.19   *Lento*   Clarinet

dolce

Strings *pp*

Then, to depict the flight by which the Zephyrs carry off Psyche to the Gardens of Eros, comes a theme which Franck borrowed from his own *Les Éolides*. The suggestion came from Duparc who realized his teacher's difficulty in arriving at a second idea to signify motion. At the Gardens Eros threatens to present himself, but not before a murmur of voices (sopranos, contraltos and divided tenors) warn Psyche of the perils of confrontation. She ignores the warnings and sees him, after which she is made to undergo a punishment (delivered by the sopranos). A long choral lament follows. Finally, she is forgiven and the two are joined in eternal bliss—an ending that does not take place in the original myth.

Understandably *Psyché* brought the composer charges of voluptuousness. D'Indy made matters worse by trying to put a Christian explanation on it, while Gustave Derepas considered it an allegory of a more Platonic kind. More recently it passed without challenge as a ballet (as did the *Variations Symphoniques*). The title given by Jean Babilée was *L'Amour et son amant* and it was produced in Paris in 1943. It is difficult to pass judgment on so ambiguous a work. Franck himself liked it 'parce qu'il ne s'y trouve pas une note sensuelle. . . .' Obviously it has not the voluptuousness of, say, Debussy's setting of Pierre Louÿs's Bilitis songs. Yet much of the music is very Wagnerian, not to say Tristanesque, especially the section which takes place in the Gardens of Eros. One of the Nabi painters, Maurice Denis, also treated the theme.

The balletic transformations of two of Franck's most important orchestral works must be taken as a refutation of Daniel Gregory Mason's claim that the composer's music was 'sedentary' and 'never danced'. By contrast the single Symphony he wrote in the last year of his life broke new ground by establishing the form in France in more solid fashion than the work of any of his contemporaries such as Lalo and Saint-Saëns. Though it is in only three movements and not the customary four, it is architecturally large and instrumentally varied. Indeed it possesses a slightly German weight and ponderousness, especially in its grave opening theme:

Ex. 20
Violas, Cellos & Basses

This melancholy theme seems anxious and interrogatory like some of the slow introductions in Beethoven. It proceeds for twenty bars and then we are plunged into a faster tempo using the same material as before and also some that is fresh. The idea of a reprise, if one understands Franck correctly, is not so much to create an early cyclical idea as to change tonalities from D minor to F minor and finally F major, in which the second subject appears. This includes a theme which is often cited as the motto theme of the Symphony, the so-called 'Faith' theme by which Franck is assumed to have expressed his affirmation. Set in the weak mediant, it is not altogether convincing. When given out by the full orchestra, with wind and brass prominent, its weakness seems accentuated. The note A, which is the pivot of the theme, recurs nine times in the first five bars, making the whole tune one of Franck's typically polarized subjects in which everything turns back on to the same note of notes. It is, however, a striking phrase and, if one can overcome this febrile impression, forms a memorable enough motto. Debussy, a stern judge, liked it and remarked: 'What smart ideas!' In view of its importance to the Symphony it is worth noting in detail:

Ex. 21

Woodwind,
Trumpets,
Violins

ff sosten.

After a brassy recapitulation the second movement, which does duty
for slow movement and *scherzo* combined, opens quietly. It begins with
a charming *Allegretto*, first given out on *pizzicato* strings and harp
(reminiscent of the *Variations Symphoniques*) then following on the cor
anglais. The choice of this instrument puzzled one of the professors at
the Conservatoire, who had the notion that it had never previously been
used in a symphony and was inappropriate to the form. He had evidently forgotten Haydn's *Philosopher* Symphony or earlier symphonies by
French composers. The cor anglais tune sounds best played at a fairly
quick tempo, even though Franck is alleged to have told Louis de Serres
that he wished it to be indicative of an ancient procession. It is perhaps
the best theme in the Symphony since it conspicuously avoids harping
on one note of the 'Faith' theme and the mincing effect of several of the
others. The middle section of this impressive movement is mostly subdued
clarinets. Incidentally Franck wrote a part for bass clarinet in this work,
an instrument less common in the symphonies of the time than the cor
anglais. He was not, however, attacked for this. The finale begins with a
brisk syncopated tune which is somewhat vitiated by its weak-beat
emphasis. Franck had a fatal penchant for accenting the last beat of the
bar, and he does it here with particularly damaging effect. What ensues
is a resumé of material from the first and second movements providing the
cyclical element once again. This time the material seems overplayed
and the climax to the movement is certainly overdone.

Reactions to Franck's Symphony were generally negative at the time.

Franck

The comments of Bellaigue and Gounod have already been mentioned (see pp. 47–8). In view of the discouraging response it is remarkable that it should have turned out to be his most popular composition—popular, that is, with the mass of concert-goers. Critics are still inclined to sneer at it, and there was a phase in the 1930s when some openly abjured it. Constant Lambert in his book *Music Ho!* described it as 'a chimerical monster, a musical Minotaur that has fortunately had no progeny'. Cecil Gray, after first acclaiming the work, later turned to Sibelius in preference, altogether disavowing his former admiration. Despite such views the Symphony has always been a favourite in England, perhaps as an antidote to the Wagnerism which was found unacceptable at the time of the two world wars. Whatever view we take there is much to commend as well as criticize in it. Without it, it is doubtful whether we should have had the later works of Chausson, Dukas, D'Indy, Dutilleux and Messiaen.

CHAPTER XI

ORATORIO, OPERA AND OTHER VOCAL FORMS

FRANCK'S vocal music, though he set much store by it, has fallen into deep disrepute, partly because it seems to us to express an outdated form of piety. Other reasons for its neglect, however, are not hard to find. For one thing he was not truly an ecclesiastical composer, yet his religious music is not sufficiently free of church sentiments to escape ambiguity. Bordes considered Franck more of an evangelical composer, while other critics have complained that his works are merely maudlin. There is certainly some truth in these charges, especially when one notes that almost all of the large religious works form a genre of their own. Part oratorio, part cantata, they are not meant to fit into the liturgy. Another reason underlying their present unpopularity is that Franck, for all his perseverance, never succeeded in writing a vocal work that comes close to his better chamber or piano works in merit. In the sphere of opera, in which he is nearly unknown, his incompetence was patent.

The first of the major vocal works was the oratorio *Ruth*, completed in September 1845 at the conclusion of what we have termed the composer's Belgian period. Taking the biblical text, and having it rearranged in fifteen parts by a mediocre poet named Alexandre Guillemin, Franck wrote for an orchestra of twenty-three and a choir of seventy. It was thus a work of considerable ambition. Moreover it avoided the Italian banalities of the day—a remarkable feat in one so young. The instrumentation is clear, showing that Franck had a firm grasp of orchestral technique from the outset of his career. Otherwise the main influence seems to be that of Berlioz, detectable in the *Chœur des Moissonneurs* and the *Marche des Moabites*. Each of these set pieces was to become relatively popular played on its own. The *Marche des Pèlerins* is also Berliozian, and the remaining choral writing is sometimes reminiscent of Schubert. The main fault with the work is its awkward plan, its general timidity. Its harmony, too, is unadventurous.

Franck

Franck did not write any further vocal works for a few years. The 1848 Revolution inspired him to write his *Chants des Trois Exilés,* a choral work in the style known as *garde nationale.* They are occasional pieces and are of no consequence in the composer's canon. The next important work was the opera *Le Valet de Ferme (The Farm-hand).* Franck, who was by this time married, was undoubtedly pressured into writing this tedious drama by his opera-conscious in-laws. It was, however, taken seriously by the composer. A tale involving the eternal triangle, it was set in eighteenth-century Ireland and unhappily made hardly any use of stage properties of the kind then so much in demand. Its libretto (written by Alphonse Royer and Gustave Vaëz, two of the nation's leading figures) turned out to be curiously deficient. Franck had once before tried his hand at opera in a little piece on the life of the seventeenth-century composer Stradella, but this had been done in his student days and had in any case not been scored for orchestra. He was thus virtually inexperienced in the theatre at the time of writing *Le Valet de Ferme,* and his lack of dramatic sense is obvious both in the music (which has no real climaxes) and the action (which is incorrigibly monotonous). Unfortunately he was also ill at the time he wrote it, or at least a good part of it. He took eighteen months over the score, much of it spent in Besançon. It is hardly surprising, therefore, that the opera never took to the boards.

This failure to break into the theatre was possibly what imposed a still longer silence on Franck's part, not broken into until 1859 when he began work on the Mass for three voices. It represents one of his very few unequivocal church works, and may again have been prompted by his new position at Sainte-Clotilde. The work is not as bad as *Le Valet de Ferme,* but it is particularly uneven in quality. That it was not finished for a great many years testifies to the difficulty Franck had with some of its sections. The most successful are the Kyrie and the Agnus Dei. The former was among the earliest sections to be finished, the latter among the last. The Kyrie is simple in form and harmonic structure and took Franck only a very short time to write. The Agnus, on the other hand, cost him a great deal of effort, and he committed the very untypical act of ripping up a preliminary version and recomposing it. The three voices used for solos in the Mass are soprano, tenor and bass, and there are some difficulties of balance with the chorus here and there. The Credo is the most complex section and the one that must have cost Franck most to complete. Its sonata form shows how determined the composer was to cling to his beloved classical principles even in a strictly liturgical work. The Sanctus and Gloria, both written in the early attempt, vary in quality. D'Indy goes as far as to label the latter 'vulgar' and to trace its ancestry to the more cliché-ridden choruses of Meyerbeer. It belonged in his opinion to what he termed the 'Hebraic' phase of French music—a damning indictment from so anti-Semitic a scholar. It is certainly bad music, and probably set a precedent for much that was worse. By its over-use of the harp and distant choir it encouraged an indulgent habit which many religious composers since have been eager to perpetuate. The notorious Panis Angelicus was added much later than the other sections and has achieved an independent popularity despite its sentimentality.

Franck wrote another work based on a biblical text in 1865. This was La Tour de Babel. It is not one of his better compositions. The chief weakness is the sameness of its sections, the lack of drama. After all, musical opportunities to depict rowdiness were built into this subject, and Franck decided to ignore them. In their place he substituted a dull dialogue between God and Man, using the Latin Vulgate as his text. The best feature of La Tour is the contrapuntal writing, now much more assured. In spite of this, however, Franck failed to find a publisher for it and it lapsed into obscurity.

The next work, like the Mass, was a long time germinating. In fact it took Franck the entire decade from 1869 to 1879. It was the nine-part oratorio Les Béatitudes, the composer's largest and most impressive vocal offering. He had long wished to set passages from the Sermon on the Mount and only lacked a guiding hand to provide him with a poetic selection. This hand eventually came from a Mme Colomb, the wife of a teacher at the Versailles lycée. Her version of the words is not especially adroit, but Franck was never one to gaze critically at his texts. In this case, however, he might have been more aware of the monotony that would inevitably ensue from setting eight blessings of similar mood and character. The work is not liturgical as the Mass was. It rather belongs to a genre not unlike that of Brahms's Requiem, to which it is very near in date. Critics have also compared it with works as far apart as Berlioz's

Grande Messe des Morts and Wagner's *Parsifal*. Yet it is not conceivable that Franck was influenced by any of these compositions. *Les Béatitudes* expresses his own saintly form of dedication and owes little if anything to any other musician.

Each *canto* in this exceedingly long work follows roughly the same plan. First of all a particular evil is set out for what it is; then comes a celestial prophecy; and finally the voice of Christ is heard in declamation. This predictable plan in itself contributes to the work's monotony, but Franck manages to vary his material here rather better than usual. A Prologue precedes the First Beatitude in which the voice of Christ is made explicit thematically. This theme Franck first entrusts to the cellos and bassoons, and it is notably plastic in invention. It occurs frequently enough to deserve quotation:

Ex. 22 *Lento ma non troppo*

The theme symbolizes Christ's mission as the dispenser of hope, charity and consolation. Seen in retrospect it becomes the chief unifying idea in the whole work, being heard in one variant or another at the conclusion of each of the succeeding sections.

The Prologue, though it makes no effort to depict the physical environment in which the Sermon is delivered, is not devoid of dramatic elements. By comparison the First Beatitude, which celebrates the poor in spirit, is rather a weak affair. Its *chœur de mauvais riches* is cast in the accent and idiom of Meyerbeer. In 6/8 time, this section does not seem particularly suited to Franck's talents, and it is only with the voice of Christ and choir of angels at the close that these talents again come to fruition. The Second Beatitude, which has as its text 'Blessed are the meek', is hardly a sufficient contrast. It is, however, well constructed in free fugal form, with the instrumentation centring upon oboes, bassoons and horns. Sections of the music seem to anticipate Chausson's Symphony of twenty years later. The ending this time is a beautifully balanced vocal quintet. Rhythmically the Second Beatitude is more interesting than the first, its syncopations marking a welcome departure for Franck. Pictorial writing is presupposed in the Third Beatitude, which blesses those who mourn. A variety of lamentations is presented—for an orphan alone in the world; for a man who has lost his wife; and for a mother bereft of her son. Following these a series of more generalized portraits emerge—such as a slave miserable at the loss of his freedom and a philosopher who has become disenchanted with his theories. All these pictures are rendered in music that is serious and dignified, each section being succeeded by repetition of the main theme.

With the Third Beatitude a dramatic peak is reached. The choir splits into five parts to evoke *les mal-aimés* of life. There is a certain Old Testament atmosphere about this section that lends it terror and agitation. Normally the choral writing is divided into two—a terrestrial and a celestial chorus. Here it is more complex, though the rhythms are slightly reminiscent of the impoverished *Mass for three voices*. A change of mood for the Fourth Beatitude—dedicated to those who hunger after righteousness—brings out the composer's chromatic obsessions. The key is his favourite B major, though the music hovers in tonality between major and minor to good effect. Also characteristic of this Beatitude are the falling sixths and sevenths that occur in profusion. It is made up of two themes, the first of which is expressively played by clarinets, horns and bassoons and represents some of Franck's most felicitous writing:

Ex. 23 *Non troppo lento*
p espress.

pp molto sostenuto

simile

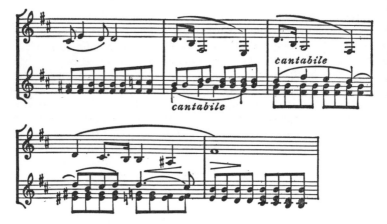

Some commentators have likened this orchestral introduction to a Wagnerian symphonic poem, but it remains unlikely that Franck was consciously influenced by events at Munich and Bayreuth.

The Fifth Beatitude sets out to justify the ways of God to Man by considering the problem of violence in the world. It is a weighty section with a heavy dose of choral writing, with the terrestrial chorus beginning rebelliously and the celestial one ending on a note of calm. This is a well balanced if rather theatrical section and carries the whole work into a larger dimension. Following it the Sixth is devoted to the pure in heart and points up the contrast between the Pharisees and those who are sincere in their beliefs. The Pharisees are represented by a choir of female voices while the Angel of Death finally passes the last judgment. By modulating into the key of F sharp at the moment when the saved are admitted to Heaven, Franck manages to suggest a withdrawal of the portals of paradise in a shimmering and highly effective piece of musical synaesthesia. A choir of angels rounds off this impressive section with a grand gesture of praise for the saints who have overcome selfishness and temptation. Much of the success of this Sixth Beatitude lies in the ornate contrapuntal writing, which d'Indy later compared to the garlands of flowers to be found in the paintings of Lippo Lippi and Fra Angelico.

Oratorio, Opera and Other Vocal Forms

In the Seventh of the series we are introduced to the character of Satan, who does not cut a very menacing figure on his initial entry and reminds us more of Gounod's portrait than of Milton's or Goethe's. He is presented in the key of C minor and Christ in that of B flat, hinting at a tonal scheme in which every character or event has its appropriate key.

The minatory aspects of Satan's character emerge far more distinctly in the Eighth and final Beatitude, which has a shape all its own. Here the dialogue between Christ and Satan rises to heroic proportions and Franck provides us with some of the best music in the entire work. Though Christ's role is limited to denial, the serenity of his music makes itself felt, while some of the choral numbers—like the famous 'O Eternal Justice'—go far towards upholding the composer's claim that this was among his finest compositions. A beautiful Mater Dolorosa from the Virgin Mary represents another summit in the piece, which ends with a last repetition of the Christ theme and a massed Hosannah from the terrestrial and celestial choirs. A brief diagram reveals how the section evolves:

1st Part

a. *Combat with Satan*—violent discourse.
b. *Chœur des Justes*—proclaiming the triumph of love.

2nd Part

Arioso of the Mater Doloroso—a plaint in which hope and love vanquish evil.

3rd Part

Retreat of Satan—Word of Christ—Hosannah *céleste*.

It will be noted that *Les Béatitudes* is not a work that can be judged from brief excerpts, yet that is how it came to be performed. Franck himself never heard the Second or Seventh sections, since they were omitted from the première. Bearing in mind his principle of tonal architecture, this was an unforgivable omission which seriously affected the work's impact. Full performances are still rare.

Notwithstanding its inferiority to *Les Béatitudes*, the cantata *Rédemption* is another important work. Written to verses by Édouard Blau in 1872 it cost Franck rather more in toil than the final result merited. The theme of the work is the gradual emergence of Man from a state of savagery to one of redemption and it is constructed in three parts. Part I presents us with the origins of human life and consists of a fifty-bar introduction followed by a long choral episode. This is probably the weakest section of the work, for we nowhere get an inkling of the barbarism evidently characteristic of Man at this stage of his development. The introduction is turgid and the chorus gives out a tamely conventional melody. An aria for an archangel is merely pallid and without interest. The whole section ends with a proclamation announcing the birth of Christ. What follows next is a symphonic interlude intended to convey the passage of time. This too is poorly constructed, especially in respect of its orchestra-tion. Basses double cellos and the sound lacks clean articulation in many places. The canonic interest of Part I is not sustained, and the texture seems to rely too much on soft pedal notes. After the interlude Part III presents the archangel once more, this time singing the praises of prayer, penitence and brotherly love. It is this section that is meant to convey the idea of redemption.

It will have been gathered that *Rédemption* is an exceedingly mixed work. That there are occasional felicities of scoring is not in doubt. The use of horns and trombones is sometimes very effective, and this has been attributed by some critics to the influence of Wagner once again. How-ever, Franck is known to have criticized Wagner's *Die Walküre* openly to his pupil Duparc in 1873, so it is unlikely that it had much influence. Other techniques of instrumentation—such as writing for the woodwind in shrill fourths—must be laid at Franck's own door. It is significant that within a year of the première (which incidentally omitted the symphonic interlude) Franck revised *Rédemption*, cutting out subtitles and casting the archangel's aria in E major in place of F sharp. A further cantata, *Rebecca*, appeared in 1881, but only the camel-drivers' chorus survived.

Franck's ventures into the field of opera have already been mentioned. His largest opus by far was not to appear until the early 1880s, however, and was predictably another failure. This was the mechanical *Hulda*, a story about the eleventh-century Aslaks of Norway based upon a play by Björnson. The libretto, by Grandmougin, did much to vitiate the work, but the subject itself was more redolent of the Second Empire than the new Republic. It was urged on Franck by his anthropologically minded son Georges. In brief it describes the trials of a young woman of the house of Hustawick who is captured by invading Aslaks. Two chieftains of the tribe, Gudleik and Gunther, quarrel over her, and she eventually arouses such jealousy as to provoke a fight in which the former is killed. Almost simultaneously another warrior, Eiolf, declares his passion for her, despite being betrothed to an Aslak girl. In Act III the king and queen of the invading tribe bemoan their situation in protracted terms. A ballet of an allegorical nature concerning the seasons is allowed to intervene in traditional fashion at this point, followed by a conspiracy to assassinate Eiolf. Meanwhile Hulda is held responsible for these misfortunes by the Aslak people, who finally drive her to her death. Despite a rousing *Marche Royale* reminiscent of *Tannhäuser* there is little in this 800-page score to activate the imagination. It alternates between bloodshed and meditation and was refused by the director of the Opéra, to whom the ballet was the sole feature of interest. Its only performances were post-humous.

The same fate overtook the last opera Franck was to write, the in-complete *Ghisèle*. This time the scene was set in the Merovingian court of Neustria and the action rather less gorged with killing. It too was mounted after the composer's death in Monaco during 1896. First it had to be completed by the pupils, and it would be idle to pronounce on work not wholly in Franck's hand. The church scenes, which were written by him, seem the best, and Augustin-Thierry's libretto is not at all bad. But opera was never Franck's forte and he would have done well to have expended his energies elsewhere.

Finally, a word or two about Franck's contribution to song seems desirable. Here it must be said that he wrote much of his output in the age of *romance*, before the *mélodie* had developed. Some of his best-known songs are *Sylphe, L'Ange et l'Enfant, Robin Gray, Souvenance* (written for Pauline Viardot), *Roses et Papillons* and *Mariage des Roses*. However, none of these gives us the feeling that Franck took careful note of French prosody. Accents tend to fall on prepositions or definite articles, anywhere in fact except the proper syllables. Probably he was less sensitive to such matters than his pupil Alexis de Castillon, who had such a short time in which to display his gifts. There can be no question about Duparc's superiority. He wrote songs far above those of Franck in merit and learned from Fauré if anyone. Possibly Franck's two best songs are

Nocturne and *Procession*, the latter conjuring up a picture of the priest and his retinue making their way across the fields on Corpus Christi Day. The accompaniments to these two songs are rather more ingenious than is the case with the remainder and there are touches of counterpoint that reveal more skill than one would think. A good example of a *fugato* occurs in the accompaniment to *Procession*:

Ex. 24. *Assez lent et solennel*

p Dieu s'avance à tra-vers les champs! Par les lan-des,

les près, les verts tail-lis de hê - - tres.

poco cresc.

In general nevertheless it must be conceded that neither Franck nor d'Indy contributed much to the evolution of the *mélodie*—a subtle art which found higher expression in the work of those other pupils mentioned and also in that of Pierre de Bréville and Sylvio Lazzari. The Parnassian poets, in whose verses we find the highest scope for French song, lay outside the sphere of Franck's unliterary sensibility and he was accordingly never to exploit what was greatest in his native muse.

APPENDICES

APPENDIX A

CALENDAR

(Figures in brackets in last column denote the age at which the person mentioned died; otherwise figures denote the age reached by the person by the end of the year concerned.)

Year	Age	Life	Contemporary Musicians
1822		César Franck, son of Nicolas-Joseph, born on Dec. 10 at Rue St Pierre, Liège.	Auber aged 40; Balfe 14; Bellini 21; Berlioz 19; Beethoven 52; Boiëldieu 47; Cherubini 62; Chopin 12; Clementi 70; Czerny 31; Dargomizhsky 9; Donizetti 25; Field 40; Glinka 19; Gossec 88; Gounod 4; Halévy 23; Hérold 31; Hummel 44; Liszt 11; Lortzing 21; Marschner 27; Mendelssohn 13; Meyerbeer 31; Rossini 30; Salieri 72; Schubert 25; Schumann 12; Spohr 38; Spontini 48; Verdi 9; Wagner 9; Weber 36.
1823	1		Lalo born, Jan. 27.
1824	2		Bruckner born, Sept. 24; Cornelius born, Dec. 24; Smetana born, March 2.
1825	3		Salieri (75) dies, May 7; Strauss (J. II) born, Oct. 25.
1826	4		Weber (40) dies, June 5.
1827	5		Beethoven (57) dies, March 26.
1828	6		Schubert (31) dies, Nov. 19.
1829	7		Gossec (95) dies, Dec. 16; Rubinstein born, Nov. 28.

Franck

Year	Age	Life	Contemporary Musicians
1830	8	Admitted to the Liège Conservatoire.	Goldmark born, May 18.
1831	9		
1832	10		Clementi (80) dies, March 10.
1833	11	Wins prize of score of Meyerbeer's *Robert le Diable*.	Brahms born, May 7; Hérold (42) dies, Jan. 19.
1834	12	First tour of Belgium as a prodigy.	Boïeldieu (59) dies, Oct. 8; Borodin born, Nov. 12.
1835	13	Writes earliest compositions for piano: *Variations brillantes* on themes from *Gustave III*; Rondo; *Variations* on themes from *Pré-aux-Clercs*; Concerto, Op. 2; Première Grande Sonate. Goes to Paris to study with Zimmermann.	Bellini (34) dies, Sept. 24; Cui born, Jan 18; Saint-Saëns born, Oct. 7.
1836	14	Writes Deuxième Grande Sonate; Fantaisie. Studies with Reicha.	
1837	15	Admitted to the Paris Conservatoire in Oct.	Balakirev born, Jan. 2; Field (55) dies, Sept. 24; Lesueur (77) dies, Oct. 6.
1838	16	Wins piano competition by playing Hummel concerto.	Bizet born, Oct. 25; Bruch born, Jan. 6.
1839	17		Mussorgsky born, March 21.
1840	18	Begins to study the organ under François Benoist.	Svendsen born, Sept. 3; Tchaikovsky born, May 7.
1841	19	Composes the three Trios, Op. 1 for piano, violin and cello.	Chabrier born, Jan. 18; Dvořák born, Sept. 8; Pedrell born, Feb. 19.
1842	20	Writes *Églogue* and duo on *God Save the King* and *Lucile*. Quits Conservatoire.	Boito born, Feb. 24; Cherubini (82) dies, March 15; Massenet born, May 12; Sullivan born, May 13.
1843	21	Composes numerous songs, including *Souvenance, Le Sylphe* and *Robin Gray*. Also writes *Stradella* and begins work on	Grieg born, June 15; Sgambati born, May 28.

Year	Age	Life	Contemporary Musicians
		Ruth. Awarded Belgian Gold Medal.	
1844	22	Completes a number of piano pieces including the *Gulistan* fantasies. Returns to Paris.	Rimsky-Korsakov born, March 18.
1845	23	*Fantaisie sur deux airs polonais* and and *Trois Petits Riens* finished.	Fauré born, May 13.
1846	24	Completes *Ruth* and gives the première. *Ce qu'on entend sur la montagne.*	Weigl (80) dies, Feb. 3.
1847	25		Mendelssohn (38) dies, Nov. 4.
1848	26	Marries and has appointment at Notre-Dame-de-Lorette. Georges born.	Donizetti (51) dies, April 8; Duparc born, Jan. 21; Parry born, Feb. 27.
1849	27		Chopin (40) dies, Oct. 17; Nicolai (39) dies, May 11.
1850	28		
1851	29	Transfers to Saint-Jean-Saint-François-au-Marais.	D'Indy born, March 27; Lortzing (48) dies, Jan. 21; Spontini (77) dies, Jan. 14.
1852	30	Completes *Le Valet de Ferme* and *Les Trois Exilés*.	Stanford born, Sept. 30.
1853	31	Suffers a slight breakdown.	
1854	32	Makes inspection of organs with Cavaillé-Coll.	Humperdinck born, Sept. 1; Janáček born, July 4.
1855	33		Chausson born, Jan. 21; Lyadov born, May 11.
1856	34		Schumann (46) dies, July 29; Sinding born, Jan. 11; Taneyev born, Nov. 25.
1857	35		Bruneau born, March 11; Elgar born, June 2; Glinka (54) dies, Feb. 15.
1858	36	Gains his post at Sainte-Clotilde. Writes *Messe Solennelle* and *Trois Motets*.	Leoncavallo born, March 8; Puccini born, June 22.
1859	37	*Trois Antiennes* for organ written.	Spohr (75) dies, Oct. 22.

Year	Age	Life	Contemporary Musicians
1860	38	*Mass for Three Voices* written. Begins work on *Six Pièces* for organ.	Albéniz born, May 29; Charpentier born, June 25; Mahler born, July 7; Wolf born, March 13.
1861	39		MacDowell born, Dec. 18; Marschner (66) dies, Dec. 14.
1862	40	Completes *Six Pièces*.	Debussy born, Aug. 27; Delius born, Jan. 29; Halévy (63) dies, March 17.
1863	41	*44 Petites Pièces* for organ or harmonium. *5 pièces* for harmonium. *La Tour de Babel*.	Mascagni born, Dec. 7.
1864	42		Meyerbeer (72) dies, May 2; Richard Strauss born, June 11.
1865	43	*Les Plaintes d'une Poupée*. Meets early pupils at Collège de Vaugirard.	Dukas born, Oct. 1; Glazunov born, Aug. 10; Sibelius born, Dec. 8.
1866	44	Meets Liszt at Sainte-Clotilde.	Busoni born, April 1.
1867	45		Granados born, July 29.
1868	46		Bantock born, Aug. 7; Rossini (76) dies, Nov. 13.
1869	47	Meets Bruckner at Notre Dame. Begins work on *Les Béatitudes*.	Berlioz (66) dies, March 8; Dargomizhky (56) dies, Jan. 17; Pfitzner born, May 5; Roussel born, April 5.
1870	48	Remains in Paris in Franco-Prussian War.	Balfe (62) dies, Oct. 20; Novák born, Dec. 5; Schmitt born, Sept. 28.
1871	49	Begins work on *Rédemption*. Commune wrecks capital.	Auber (89) dies, May 12.
1872	50	Completes *Rédemption*, also several songs. *Panis Angelicus* and *Veni Creator*. Professor at Conservatoire.	Scriabin born, Jan. 6; Vaughan Williams born, Oct. 12.
1873	51	Transcribes *Prélude, Fugue et Variation* for piano.	Rachmaninov born, April 1; Reger born, March 19.
1874	52	Interlude for *Rédemption*.	Cornelius (50) dies, Oct. 26;

Year	Age	Life	Contemporary Musicians
			Holst born, Sept. 21; Schoenberg born, Sept. 13.
1875	53		Bizet (37) dies, June 3; Ravel born, March 7.
1876	54	Writes *Les Éolides* at Azilles.	Falla born, Nov. 23.
1877	55		Dohnányi born, July 27.
1878	56	Composes *Trois Pièces* for Guilmant, played at the Trocadéro.	
1879	57	Completes *Les Béatitudes*. Writes the Piano Quintet.	Bridge born, Feb. 27; Ireland born, Aug. 13; Medtner born, Dec. 24; Respighi born, July 9; Cyril Scott born, Sept. 27.
1880	58	Given a laurel wreath by the Conservatoire.	Bloch born, July 24; Offenbach (61) dies, Oct. 4; Pizzetti born, Sept. 20.
1881	59	*Rébecca* finished.	Bartók born, March 25; Miaskovsky born, April 20; Mussorgsky (42) dies, March 28; Vieuxtemps (61) dies, June 6.
1882	60	*Le Chasseur Maudit* completed. *Hulda* begun.	Kodály born, Dec. 16; Malipiero born, March 16; Raff (60) dies, June 25; Stravinsky born, June 17; Symanowski born, Oct. 6.
1883	61		Bax born, Nov. 6; Casella born, July 25; Wagner (70) dies, Feb. 13; Webern born, Dec. 3rd.
1884	62	*Les Djinns* written. *Prélude, Choral et Fugue* and *Nocturne*.	Smetana (60) dies, May 12.
1885	63	Made Chevalier of the Legion of Honour. Completes *Hulda*. *Danse lente*. *Variations Symphoniques*.	Berg born, Feb. 7.
1886	64	Writes Violin Sonata, also *Prélude, Aria et Final*. Begins Symphony.	Liszt (75) dies, July 31.
1887	65	Begins *Psyché*.	Borodin (53) dies, Feb. 16.
1888	66	Finishes *Psyché* and the Symphony	

phony. Starts work on *Ghisèle.*
Psaume CL. La Procession,
Hymne and *Six Duos.*

1889 67 Writes the Quartet. Also
L'Organiste.

1890 68 Completes the *Trois Chorals.*
Dies of pleurisy following a
street accident, Nov. 8.

Albéniz aged 30; Balakirev 53;
Bantock 22; Bartók 9; Berg 5;
Bloch 10; Boito 48; Brahms 57;
Bridge 11; Bruch 52; Bruckner
64; Bruneau 33; Busoni 24;
Chabrier 49; Charpentier 30;
Chausson 35; Cui 55; Debussy
28; Delius 28; Dohnányi 13;
Dukas 25; Duparc 42; Dvořák
49; Elgar 33; Falla 14; Fauré
45; Glazunov 25; Gounod 72;
Granados 22; Grieg 47; Holst
16; Humperdinck 36; d'Indy
39; Ireland 11; Janáček 36;
Kodály 8; Lalo 67; Leoncavallo
32; Liadov 35; Macdowell 29;
Mahler 30; Malipiero 8; Mas-
cagni 27; Massenet 48; Medtner
11; Miaskovsky 9; Novák 20;
Parry 42; Pedrell 49; Pfitzner 21;
Pizzetti 10; Puccini 32; Rach-
maninov 17; Ravel 15; Reger
17; Rimsky-Korsakov 46;
Roussel 21; Saint-Saëns 55;
Schmitt 20; Schoenberg 16;
Scott 11; Scriabin 15; Sibelius
25; Sinding 34; Stanford 38;
Johann Strauss II 61; Richard
Strauss 26; Stravinsky 8; Suk
16; Sullivan 48; Svendsen 50;
Taneyev 34; Tchaikovsky 50;
Vaughan Williams 18; Verdi
77; Wolf 30.

APPENDIX B

PIANO SOLO

Églogue (Hirten-Gedicht), Op. 3 (1842).
Grand Caprice, Op. 5 (1843).
Souvenir d'Aix-la-Chapelle, Op. 7 (1843).
4 songs of Schubert transcribed, Op. 8 (1844).
Ballade, Op. 9 (1844).
Piano solo with accompaniment for string quartet, Op. 10 (1844).
First *Fantaisie* on Dalyrac's *Gulistan*, Op. 11 (1844).
Second *Fantaisie* on Dalyrac's *Gulistan*, Op. 12 (1844).
Fantaisie, Op. 13 (1844).
Fantaisie sur deux airs polonais, Op. 15 (1845).
Trois Petits Riens, Op. 16 (1845).
Les Plaintes d'une Poupée (1865).
Prélude, Choral et Fugue (1884).
Danse Lente (1885).
Prélude, Aria et Final (1886-7).

PIANO (FOUR HANDS)

Duo on *God Save the King*, Op. 4 (1842).
Duo on *Lucille*, Op. 17 (1846).

PIANO AND VIOLIN

Andante quietoso, Op. 6 (1843).
Duo concertant sur Gulistan, Op. 14 (1844).
Sonata in A major (1886).

CHAMBER WORKS

Trois Trios concertants, for piano, violin and cello, Op. 1 (1841).
Fourth Trio for piano, violin and cello, Op. 2 (1842).
Quintet in F minor for piano and strings (1878-9).
Quartet in D major (1889).

Franck

SONGS

Ninon (de Musset) (1843).
L'Émir de Bengador (Méry) (1843).
Le Sylphe (Dumas) (1843).
Robin Gray (Florian) (1843).
Aimer (Méry) (1843).
Souvenance (Chateaubriand) (1846).
L'Ange et L'Enfant (Reboul) (1846).
Les Trois Exilés (1852).
Le Garde d'Honneur (1859).
Le Mariage des Roses (David) (1871).
Passez, Passez Toujours (Hugo) (1872).
Roses et Papillons (Hugo) (1872).
Lied (Paté) (1873).
Le Vase Brisé (Sully-Prudhomme) (1879).
Nocturne (de Fourcaud) (1884).
La Procession (Brizeux) (1888).
Les Cloches du Soir (Daudet) (1888).
Pour les victimes. S'il est un charmant gazon (Hugo).

CHOIR

Hymne for four male voices (Racine) (1888).
Six duos pour chœur à voix égales (1888).
Le Premier Sourire de Mai (for three female voices) (Wilder) (1888).

SACRED MUSIC

— *Ruth, églogue biblique* for soloists, choir and orchestra (1843–6).
Messe Solennelle for bass solo and organ (1858).
O Salutaris, for soprano and tenor (1858).
Trois Motets (1858):
    1. *O Salutaris* for soprano and choir.
    2. *Ave Maria* for soprano and bass.
    3. *Tantum ergo* for bass.
Mass for three voices (soprano, tenor and bass, with organ, harp, cello and bass
    accompaniment), Op. 12 (1860).
Ave Maria for soprano, tenor and bass (1863).
— *La Tour de Babel*, short oratorio for soloists, choir and orchestra (1863).
Trois Offertoires (1871):
    1. *Quae est ista.*
    2. *Domine Deus in simplicitate.*

3. *Dextera Domini.*

Domine non secundum for soprano, tenor and bass (1871).

Quare fremuerunt gentes for three voices, organ and bass (1871).

Panis Angelicus for tenor, organ, harp, cello and bass (1872).

— *Rédemption*, cantata for soprano, choir and orchestra (Blau) (1871–2).

Veni, Creator for tenor and bass (1872).

Les Béatitudes, oratorio for soloists, choir and orchestra in eight parts (Colomb) (1869–79).

— *Rébecca, scène biblique* for soloists, choir and orchestra (Collin) (1881).

— *Psaume CL* for choir, orchestra and organ (1888).

ORGAN OR HARMONIUM

Andantino (1858).

Trois Antiennes for grand organ (1859).

Six Pièces for grand organ, Op. 16 (1860–2):
1. *Fantaisie* in C.
2. *Grand Pièce Symphonique.*
3. *Prélude, fugue et variation.*
4. *Pastorale.*
5. *Prière.*
6. *Final.*

Quasi Marcia for harmonium, Op. 22 (1862).

Quarante-quatre Petites Pièces for organ or harmonium (1863).

Cinq Pièces for harmonium (1863).

Offertoire for harmonium based on a Breton air (1871).

Prélude, fugue et variation for harmonium or piano (1873).

Trois Pièces for grand organ (1878):
1. *Fantaisie.*
2. *Cantabile.*
3. *Pièce héroïque.*

Andantino for grand organ (1889).

Préludes et Prières of Alkan arranged for organ (1889).

L'Organiste, fifty-nine pieces for harmonium (1889–90).

Trois Chorals for grand organ (1890).

ORCHESTRAL MUSIC

Ce qu'on entend sur la montagne (Hugo) (1846).

Symphonic interlude for *Rédemption* (1874).

Les Éolides (de Lisle) (1876).

Franck

Le Chasseur Maudit (Bürger) (1882).
Les Djinns (Hugo) (1884).
Variations Symphoniques for piano and orchestra (1885).
Psyché, symphonic poem for choir and orchestra (1887–8).
Symphony in D minor (1886–8).

OPERA

Stradella, unpublished opera in three acts (1843).
Le Valet de Ferme, *opéra-comique* in three acts (Royer and Vaëz) (1852).
Hulda, opera in four acts and epilogue (Grandmougin, after Björnson) (1882–1885).
Ghisèle, lyric drama in four acts (Augustin-Thierry) (1888–90).

APPENDIX C

Alkan, alias Valentin Morhange (1813–88), prodigious pianist and composer for the piano who was a judge at one of Franck's early examinations at the Paris Conservatoire. A friend of Liszt, he met an unusual death by reaching for a copy of the Talmud and bringing the entire bookcase down upon his head.

Auber, Louis (1782–1871), composer of operas including the very successful *Fra Diavolo* and for many years Director of the Paris Conservatoire. He was an eager patron of the Opéra-Comique.

Benoît, Camille (1851–1923), a pupil of Franck who none the less preferred to take up a career in art rather than music. He became a curator at the Louvre and a propagandist for Wagner. His works include an *Eleison* for solo voices, choir and orchestra.

Berlioz, Hector (1803–69), French composer born near Grenoble. Won the Prix de Rome after repeated attempts and went on to write the *Symphonie Fantastique, Harold en Italie, Grande Messe des Morts* and other masterpieces.

Bizet, Georges (1838–75), briefly a pupil of Franck's at the Paris Conservatoire though not a member of his circle. Composer of *Carmen* and *Les Pêcheurs de Perles*, he died young and unfulfilled.

Boëly, Alexandre (1785–1858), probably the first of the 'symphonic' organists, he ruled over the organ at St Germain l'Auxerrois. He died before he could have influenced Franck very much, but his style of playing laid the foundations of Franck's later works.

Bordes, Charles (1863–1909), one of Franck's most prominent pupils, he also became a founder of the Schola Cantorum and a fine choral conductor. Interested in Basque music, he also edited works by the sixteenth-century polyphonists. His own music included songs to poems by Verlaine and an unfinished opera, *Les Trois Vagues*.

Bréville, Pierre de (1861–1949), one of the last of Franck's pupils, a prolific song writer and composer of chamber music. He was professor of counterpoint at the Schola and wrote a censored opera entitled *Éros Vainqueur*.

Bruneau, Alfred (1857–1934), had a great reputation in his day for naturalistic operas, of which he wrote thirteen. The most famous are *Le Rêve* and

L'Ouragan. He suffered as a result of his close collaboration with Zola. His sympathies were always directed towards the Franck circle.

Cahen, Albert (1846–1903), a pupil of Franck, he was mainly interested in the lighter kind of opera. His career as a musician was largely unsuccessful. Brother of Count Louis Cahen d'Anvers and friend of Guy de Maupassant.

Castillon, Alexis de (1838–73), a very promising Franck pupil who unfortunately died as a result of ill-health incurred in the Franco-Prussian War. He wrote a fine Piano Concerto and Piano Quintet. Also known for his early interest in the *mélodie.*

Chabrier, Emmanuel (1841–94), rumbustious companion of Franck's, he delivered his friend's funeral oration in 1890. Composer of the opera *Gwendoline*, he was also fanatically devoted to Wagner's music. Best known for his Spanish rhapsody, *España.*

Chausson, Ernest (1855–99), perhaps the most talented of Franck's pupils. Wrote a splendid *Poème* for violin and orchestra and also a full-length symphony. A generous patron to struggling musicians, he was killed in a cycling accident at one of his estates.

Cherubini, Luigi (1760–1842), Director of the Paris Conservatoire while Franck was a student there, he was chiefly revered for his operas. A serious disciplinarian, he imposed Italian ways on French music and was a particular enemy of Berlioz.

Colonne, Édouard (1838–1910), famous French conductor who did much to popularize Wagner, Berlioz and Debussy. He founded the Association Artistique des Concerts Colonne in 1875. Not a good interpreter of Franck, he was responsible for the botched performance of *Rédemption.*

Coquard, Arthur (1848–1910), friend of Duparc and d'Indy, he was one of Franck's earliest pupils at the Collège de Vaugirard. He wrote a colourful opera entitled *Le Troupe Jolicœur* and encouraged many *auditeurs* to attend Franck's classes at the Conservatoire. Also worked as secretary to Martel in the Senate and was responsible for getting Franck a decoration.

David, Félicien (1810–76), composer of oriental fantasies such as *Le Désert* and *Lalla Roukh.* The former work had a pronounced influence on Franck, especially on his cantata *Ruth.*

Debussy, Claude (1862–1918), briefly a captive pupil in Franck's organ class, never wished to study with him though he wrote about him in complimentary fashion in his book *Monsieur Croche.*

Dukas, Paul (1865–1935), never an actual pupil of Franck, but a great admirer.

Appendix C—Personalia

He taught at the Conservatoire and composed on a small but very successful plane. Among his works are *L'Apprenti Sorcier*, a symphony and a sonata. He was also a critic.

Duparc, Henri (1848–1933), pupil of Franck and superb song-writer. Acted as secretary to the Société Nationale until his health broke down. Wrote only sixteen songs and then suffered a mysterious creative inhibition. Also composed a symphonic poem, *Lénore*.

Fauré, Gabriel (1845–1924), pioneer of the French *mélodie* with songs like *Lydia* and *Après un Rêve*. Also worthy of note as the writer of many neglected piano pieces modelled on Chopin. He wrote two operas and eventually became Director of the Paris Conservatoire in succession to Dubois in 1905.

Franck, Georges (1848–1910), pompous and opinionated son of Franck whom he constantly urged to write opera. He was responsible for suggesting *Hulda* and arranged for the completion of *Ghisèle*. He was a teacher at the Lycée Lakanal and university lecturer.

Franck, Nicolas-Joseph (1796–1871), tyrannical father of the composer. In Franck's early days Nicolas-Joseph arranged all his concerts and appropriated most of his fees. It was on account of his greed and ineptitude that César had so prolonged a period as an unsuccessful virtuoso.

Fumet, Dynam-Victor (1867–1949), pupil of Franck who was also an anarchist friend of Bakunin. He was dismissed from the Conservatoire for revolutionary activities, but later made a success as organist of the Oratorian College at Juilly. Travelled in South America and composed somewhat in the style of Satie. He left many religious works, including a Requiem (1948).

Gounod, Charles (1818–93), operatic composer whose only real success was *Faust*. Became a friend of Franck's in their young days but was later estranged from him. Went to England during the Franco-Prussian War and became known as a prolific writer of songs and choral pieces. His *Rédemption* (to his own text) was written some ten years after Franck's version.

Guilmant, Alexandre (1837–1911), probably France's best organist in his day and a founder of the Schola Cantorum. He played Franck's *Trois Pièces* at the Trocadéro and enjoyed cordial relations with him. His style of playing eventually went out of favour.

Habeneck, F.-A. (1781–1849), violinist and teacher of Franck at the Paris Conservatoire. He was a keen concert organizer and mounted a variety of orchestral concerts at the Conservatoire which helped to form Franck's taste.

Halévy, Fromental (1799–1862), composer of operas, notably the successful *La Juive*. Taught at the Conservatoire, where he influenced Bizet, who married his daughter Geneviève.

Holmès, Augusta (1847–1903), Irish pupil of Franck who was also a devotee of Wagner's music. Franck was rumoured to have fallen in love with her and to have written his Piano Quintet to express his feelings for her. Her own music was made up of operas, of which the best is known *La Montagne Noire*, and patriotic odes. She was an ardent nationalist, at home and abroad, and had a liaison with the poet Catulle Mendès.

Indy, Vincent d' (1851–1931), stern-minded pupil of Franck's class from 1872 onwards. Became Director of the Schola Cantorum and secretary of the Société Nationale. As a composer, he was inclined to aridity, but he wrote prolifically in the field of opera, symphonic and chamber music. His best opera is probably *L'Étranger* and his *Symphonie Cévenole* was among the earliest works to use the piano as a *concertante* instrument within the symphony.

Lalo, Édouard (1823–92), composer of the opera *Le Roi d'Ys*, he was also a keen chamber-music enthusiast at a time when that art was unpopular. He played the viola in the Armingaud Quartet and probably encouraged Franck to write his own chamber works.

Lazzari, Sylvio (1857–1944), little-known pupil of Franck. He was highly talented and wrote an extremely contentious opera called *La Lépreuse*. Late in life he became the first composer to use cinematic effects on the opera stage in his *La Tour de Feu* (1924). His settings of Verlaine and other poets are much neglected.

Lefébure-Wély, A. (1817–69), one of the greatest organists of the nineteenth century, he influenced Franck by his manner of playing. Franck dedicated one of his *Six Pièces* to him.

Lekeu, Guillaume (1870–94), immensely gifted last pupil of Franck. He was Belgian and almost won the Belgian Prix de Rome. His works are highly advanced and contrapuntal, yet have an expressive effect. He is best known for his Violin Sonata, but he also wrote much other chamber music, including a *Quatuor inachevé* of huge dimension. His death came early, from typhoid, as a result of drinking contaminated sherbet.

Lemmens, Jacques-Nicolas (1823–81), another important virtuoso organist and fellow Belgian. It was said of him that he played better with his feet than most organists did with their hands. Franck heard him play and was greatly impressed.

Appendix C—Personalia

Liszt, Franz (1811–86), Hungarian-born composer and pianist. His most notable works are the *Faust Symphony* and B minor Sonata. His encouragement of Franck in the days of his Belgian tours and Paris début was of signal importance. Each man wrote a symphonic poem on Hugo's *Ce qu'on entend sur la montagne.*

Magnard, Albéric (1865–1914), a pupil of d'Indy rather than Franck, but very much influenced by the latter's ideas. Rather an ascetic composer, he wrote several operas and a variety of chamber music. Was shot by the Germans in 1914 while defending his house at Baron-sur-Oise.

Massenet, Jules (1842–1912), hard-working and famous opera-composer. Best-known works are *Manon, Werther* and *Cendrillon.* Was a senior professor at the Conservatoire where he took away many of Franck's prospective pupils.

Mendelssohn, Felix (1809–47), German composer famous for his 'Scotch' and 'Italian' symphonies. His connection with Franck was tenuous, but he was markedly interested in the Trios Franck wrote and was about to sanction a performance of them when he died.

Meyerbeer, Giacomo (1791–1864), scion of 'grand opera' in France. Lent a certain encouragement to Franck in his younger days and was a source of influence in many of Franck's choral works. Franck was given a copy of his opera *Robert le Diable* as a prize at the Royal Liège Conservatoire.

Pasdeloup, Jules (1819–87), prominent French conductor and musician responsible for the Société des Jeunes Artistes. He did much to assist Bizet and Saint-Saëns, but his treatment of Franck was never remarkable. His greatest error was when he mishandled the second performance of the *Variations Symphoniques* by creating a faulty string entry in the last section.

Pierné, Gabriel (1863–1937), pupil of Franck's who wrote a great quantity of music as well as winning the Prix de Rome. He followed Franck at the organ of Sainte-Clotilde from 1890 to 1898 after which he took over the direction of the Concerts Colonne. His output covered every sector, but he is perhaps best known for his contribution to *opéra-comique*, notably in *Sophie Arnould* and *Fragonard.*

Ravel, Maurice (1875–1937), never a pupil of Franck's and a man rather opposed to the Franck school. His String Quartet (1905) nevertheless betrays a Franckist concern with cyclical form. Best known for his contribution to the Ballet Russe and for his difficult but rewarding piano pieces.

Reicha, Antonín (1770–1836), taught Franck privately while he was a professor at the Conservatoire. Matriculated in company with Beethoven at Bonn and was a member of the Electoral orchestra there. Was a mystic with interests in philosophy and may have influenced Franck in this direction. His opera *Natalie* was a failure.

Ropartz, Guy (1864–1955), one of Franck's most faithful pupils who went on to become head of the Strasbourg and Nancy Conservatoires. He composed five symphonies, an attractive *Sérénade Champêtre* and an opera called *Le Pays*. Was especially equipped as an orchestrator. It was his insistence that interested Ysaÿe in Franck's music.

Rousseau, Samuel-Alexandre (1853–1904), pupil of Franck's who won the Prix de Rome. Also studied with Bazin. His main interest lay in opera and he wrote *Dinorah* while still a student. Among his later ventures was *La Cloche du Rhin*. He assisted in the writing of *Hulda* and the completion of *Ghisèle*.

Saint-Saëns, Camille (1835–1921), composer of *Samson et Dalila* and *Étienne Marcel*. Never an intimate friend of Franck's, he none the less took an interest in the circle's activities. He, too, was reputed to have been in love with Augusta Holmès and it was he who ironically gave the première of Franck's Piano Quintet.

Spontini, Luigi (1774–1851), an Italian who settled in Paris in 1803. His best-known works were for the stage, the operas *La Vestale* (1807) and *Fernand Cortez* (1909). He attended the first performance of Franck's *Ruth*.

Thomas, Ambroise (1811–96), a director of the Conservatoire. It was under his administration that Franck was professor of organ. He nevertheless disliked Franck's music and disapproved of his teaching composition. He was reputedly sardonic about Franck's Symphony. Among his own works *Mignon* has survived best.

Tournemire, Charles (1870–1939), briefly a pupil of Franck before studying with Widor. A shy man, he did little to promote his own considerable works. These include nine symphonies and a curious symphonic poem entitled *Les Combats de l'Idéal* which portrays Faust and Don Quixote. He succeeded Pierné at the organ of Sainte-Clotilde. Was found dead in the street at Arcachon in 1939.

Viardot, Pauline (1821–1910), dramatic soprano and sister to the immortal Malibran. She became a literary hostess of international renown and companion of the Russian novelist Turgenev. It was for her that Franck wrote his song *Souvenance*. Her daughter Marianne was briefly engaged to Fauré.

Appendix C—Personalia

Vierne, Louis (1870–1937), organist who studied for a very short time under Franck and whose interest remained with the organ. He wrote numerous organ symphonies which were probably influenced by Franck's *Chorals* and died after giving a recital at Notre Dame in 1937.

Wailly, Paul de (1854–1926), lesser-known pupil of Franck's who was put to an extremely rigorous test in his lessons. He endured the pressures and went on to write religious works very much like those of his teacher, the best known being *L'Apôtre* (1924).

Widor, Charles-Marie (1845–1937), brilliant symphonic organist who took over Franck's post at the Conservatoire after his death, inheriting several of his pupils. He was a more adventurous player of the instrument than Franck and became notable for his treatise on orchestration, which was of great value to Ravel and others.

Ysaÿe, Eugène-Auguste (1858–1931), Belgian violinist. He was professor at the Brussels Conservatoire from 1886 to 1898 and conductor of the Cincinnati Orchestra from 1918 to 1921. He founded the Ysaÿe Quartet in 1888. He gave the first performance of Franck's Violin Sonata, which was dedicated to him.

APPENDIX D

SELECT BIBLIOGRAPHY

Baldensperger, F., 'César Franck, l'artiste et son œuvre.' (Paris, Éditions du Courrier Musical, 15th May 1901.)

Benoît, C., 'César Franck.' (Paris, *La Revue Bleue,* 1890.) 'César Franck.' (Paris, *La Revue et Gazette Musicale,* 1890.)

Bordes, C., 'Le Sentiment Religieux dans la Musique d'Église de Franck.' (Paris, Éditions du Courrier Musical, 1st Nov. 1904.)

Borren, C. van den, L'Œuvre Dramatique de César Franck.' (Brussels, Schott, 1907.)

Bréville, P. de, 'Les Fioretti de César Franck.' (Paris, *Mercure de France,* Sept. 1935/Jan. 1936/July 1937/Jan. 1938.)

Buenzod, E., 'César Franck.' (Paris, Éditions Seghers, 1966.)

Cardus, N., 'Ten Composers.' (London, Cape, 1945, rev. 1958.)

Chausson, E., 'César Franck.' (Paris, le Passant, 1891.)

Closson, E., 'Les Origines Germaniques de César Franck.' (Paris, S.I.M., 1913.)

Colling, A., 'César Franck ou le Concert Spirituel.' (Paris, Julliard, 1951.)

Cooper, M., 'French Music from the death of Berlioz to the death of Fauré.' (London, O.U.P., 1951.)

Coquard, A., 'César Franck.' (Paris, *Le Monde,* 1904.)

Cortot, A., 'French Piano Music, Vol. I.' Translated by Hilda Andrews. (London, O.U.P., 1932.)

Davies, L., 'César Franck and His Circle.' (London, Barrie & Jenkins, 1970.)

Dawson, R. V., 'Beethoven and César Franck.' (London, *Music and Letters,* Vol. XI, No. 2, April 1930.)

Dean, W., 'César Franck.' (London, Novello.)

Debay, V., 'César Franck.' (Paris, Éditions du Courrier Musical, 15th Nov. and 1st Dec. 1900.)

Appendix D—Select Bibliography

Debussy, C., 'Monsieur Croche—anti-dilettante.' Translated by Langland Davies. (London, Dover Books, 1960).

Demuth, N., 'César Franck.' (London, Harrap, 1949.)

Derepas, G., 'César Franck.' (Paris, Fischbacher, 1897.)

Destranges, E., 'L'Œuvre Lyrique de César Franck.' (Paris, Fischbacher, 1896.)

Dufourcq, N., 'César Franck.' (Paris, La Colombe, 1949.)

Emmanuel, M., 'César Franck, étude critique.' (Paris, Laurens, 1930.)

Gallois, J., 'César Franck.' (Paris, Éditions du Seuil, 1966.)

Hervey, A., 'French Music of the Nineteenth Century.' (London, Grant Richards, 1903.)

Hill, E. B., 'Modern French Music.' (Boston, Houghton-Mifflin, 1924.)

Horton, J., 'The Chamber Music of César Franck.' (London, O.U.P., Musical Pilgrim Series, 1943.)

Indy, V. d', 'César Franck.' (Paris, Alcan, 1906.)

Jardillier, R., 'La Musique de Chambre de César Franck.' (Paris, Librairie Mellottée, 1929.)

Kunel, M., 'César Frank, l'homme et l'œuvre.' (Paris, Grasset, 1947.)

Landormy, P., 'La Musique Française de Franck à Debussy.' (Paris, Gallimard, 1944.)

Pearsall, R., 'The Serene Anxiety of César Franck.' (London, *Music Review*, Vol. 27, No. 2, May 1966.)

Pitrou, R., 'De Gounod à Debussy.' (Paris, Albin Michel, 1957.)

Roberts, W., 'César Franck.' (London, *Music and Letters*, Vol. III, No. 4, Oct. 1922.)

Ropartz, G., 'César Franck.' (Paris, *Revue Internationale de Musique*, June 1898.)

Rudder, M., 'César Franck.' (Turnhout, Brepols 1920.)

Seitz, A., 'Le Génie de César Franck.' (Paris, *Monde Musical*, Oct. 30th 1904.)

Franck

Tiersot, J., 'Un demi-siècle de Musique Française.' (Paris, Alcan, 1918.)
Tournemire, C., 'César Franck.' (Paris, Delagrave, 1931.)

Vallas, L., 'La Véritable Histoire de César Franck.' (Paris, Flammarion, 1955.)

Wailly, P. de, 'César Franck.' (Paris, Durand, 1922.)

INDEX

Index

Index